The whole art of war consists
in getting at what is on the
other side of the hill.
—Duke of Wellington

I can't get at the enemy here.
He is too well dug in. So I'm
laying siege to San Diego.
When the pressures get too
intense, then we will see what
comes up over the hill.
—Mack Bolan, THE EXECUTIONER

THE EXECUTIONER: SAN DIEGO SIEGE

An original Pinnacle Books edition, published
for the first time anywhere.

First printing, November 1972

Printed in the United States of America

PINNACLE BOOKS,
A Division of Carlyle Communications, Inc.
116 East 27 Street, New York, N.Y. 10016

Dedicated with admiration to
that gutsy community of journalists
referred to as "investigative
reporters"—and especially to
a young Indiana journalist,
Lee Aschoff. *Fiat lux*, Lee.

dp

PROLOGUE

The tall man in midnight combat garb stood in stark silhouette on the high ground atop Point Loma, gazing broodingly upon the sprawl and sweep of California's oldest city. Coronado and the impressive Naval Air Station lay directly ahead, Lindbergh Field and the Marine Base slightly to the north, the complex of seagoing navy activities spilling off toward the south bay. Backdrop to it all was the old city herself with her hills and freeways and suburban clusters—"Dago" to generations of servicemen, *San Diego* to those who proudly loved her and made their homes in the sunny, smog-free environment . . . "hellground" to the tall man in black who quietly contemplated his next area of operations.

He was Mack Bolan, Mafia-fighter *extraordinaire,* the one man army who had already become legend in the world's annals of crime.

7

This time, however, he was not alone.

Another man moved into silhouette against the city's lights—a shorter man, heavier, powerfully built.

The meeting had been pre-arranged. The greetings, though restrained almost to the point of stiff formality, were nonetheless warmly emotional in undertone.

"You got my message," the short man said, for openers.

"I wish I hadn't," the other murmured.

"Sure, I know. But . . . well, you said it yourself once or twice. A life without challenge is no life at all. I couldn't stay up there boy-scouting while all this—"

"Okay," Bolan interrupted. He was not a man to spend much time on small talk, but the voice was tired, concerned, and admiring all at once as he added, "You're looking good, Pol. Dropped a few pounds, eh?"

"Yeh." The man patted his belly. "Few inches, too. You look as mean as ever. Even with the pretty new face. Brantzen did a good job."

"They got Brantzen," Bolan declared coldly.

"Yeah, I heard."

"They'll get us all, eventually. You have to know that, Pol."

"Sure, I know that," the other agreed. "In the meantime. . . ."

Bolan sighed. "Okay. What's the big smell?"

"That town down there. They call it 'the city around a park,' or words to that effect."

"So?"

"They should call it 'the town that Uncle built,' meaning Uncle Sam. Between the military bases

8

and the defense contractors, it's the highest federal-impact area in the nation, dollar for dollar."

"Go on," Bolan prompted.

"Well you know what federal dollars mean."

"The city built around a picnic," Bolan replied quietly.

"Yeah. And also the city with a Mexican border. Plus one of the world's ten greatest natural harbors."

The man in black again sighed. "I don't have this town on my hit parade, Pol. They're too well covered here. There's no battleground down there, no combat stretch. San Diego doesn't have skin lesions—it's got cancer of the gut. I can't carve it out without removing a lot of good tissue along with the rot."

"That's exactly the problem," the other man muttered. "An old friend of ours is caught up in that rot down there."

"Who's that?"

"Howlin' Harlan Winters."

Sure. Colonel Harlan P. Winters—Howlin' Harlan or Howlie to his troops, a soldier's soldier, once top-dog of the elite Penetration Teams in Vietnam.

Bolan said, "I heard that he'd retired."

"Yeah. Kicked him up to Brigadier and right out the goddam door."

"That happens to good soldiers sometimes," Bolan mused. "Especially when they get too good."

"Well, he's in a hell of a mess now."

"A mob mess?"

"That's the smell I get. I stumbled onto the thing up in Frisco, sheer accident. He's in deep

9

shit, Sarge—and he needs a guy with a big shovel."

"Meaning the Executioner."

"Yeah."

Bolan's shoulders drooped forward in an almost imperceptible movement and the eyes turned to ice as they returned to a sweep of the crescent coastline of San Diego Bay. He told his companion, "I just came from a messy one, Pol."

"Yeah, I know, I heard. They were even trying to tie you into an assassination attempt on the President. I knew that was pure bullshit the minute I heard it."

"This one could get even messier," the Executioner declared. "I brought quite a bit of intel away from that Washington sweep. Enough to know that . . . well, I can't just blitz into San Diego. And especially not for Howlin' Harlan."

"You know something about him I don't," the other man decided.

"Maybe. Did he ask for me, Pol?"

"Hell no. He doesn't even know I'm into it, yet."

"Then how . . . ?"

"I bumped into him up in Frisco. Looked terrible, scared outta his skull when he recognized me. Said he was on a business trip. Had a chick with him, introduced her as his niece. We had a drink together, the three of us. Small talked, that's all, then they split. Next day the chick looked me up, with SOS written all over her. Now is the time for all old troopers to come to the aid of the C.O. That was her message. You see, he—"

"Save it for a full briefing," Bolan suggested. "You split for now. Meet me again tomorrow—same time, same place."

10

The other man displayed a tense smile. "It's a go, then."

"A tentative go. I want to scout the terrain a bit before I commit myself."

"Okay, but look out for these San Diego cops. I hear they're pretty savvy."

Bolan knew about the San Diego cops. Many of them, especially higher echelon types, were ex-feds who'd decided they could do a better job under local colors. Which usually meant that something was rotten in fedville. He told his friend, "Yeah, I'll watch it. Now split. Too long already."

"Gadgets wants into this one, too," the other man said, smiling soberly.

Bolan gave a resigned sigh and replied, "Okay. Tell him I said welcome aboard. I'll need every talent he's got."

The smile grew. "The death squad is reborn."

"Not quite," Bolan said.

"Yeah, you're right, not quite."

Rosario "the Politician" Blancanales, along wih Herman "Gadgets" Schwarz had fought beside Bolan in Vietnam . . . and also in Los Angeles with seven others . . . the Executioner's "Death Squad." Of the nine, only Pol and Gadgets survived.

The two men locked eyes for a moment, and there was no disguising the pain which passed between them. Then Blancanales punched his old friend lightly on the shoulder and faded quickly into the darkness.

The entire meeting had consumed less than two minutes.

But the man in black remained on Point Loma for another half-hour, pushing an infinity of ideas through his combat-conditioned mind, re-examining his priorities, re-assessing the implications and directions of this eternal damned war of his. He was realist enough to realize that it could not, in fact, be an eternal war . . . it simply seemed that way. He could survive just so many firefights, elude just so many cops, live just so long.

And he had to make every breath of life count for something positive.

As for a resurrection of the Death Squad, even a partial resurrection . . . he had vowed never again to take on allies, never again to deliberately place friendly lives on his firing line. There had been much too many live sacrifices upon the altars of the Executioner's crusades. And yet . . . Pol and Gadgets were living in some sort of purgatory, at best. If they wished to come out and meet their fates head-on. . .

It was no private damned war.

It had started that way, of course . . . private . . . but not a war, not in the real sense. It had begun as a simple quest for personal justice. Sergeant Mack Bolan, much decorated hero of a seemingly endless war in Southeast Asia, had come home from that combat theatre solely to bury his parents and teenage sister—victims of another sort of ferocity—and to arrange for the care of his kid brother, the lone survivor of that tragedy at home.

But then Sgt. Bolan learned that there was more to the story than was mentioned in the official police report. Ailing steelworker Sam Bolan, Mack's father, had been in a financial squeeze. He had borrowed money at appallingly usurious rates from a local loan company, one which turned out to be operating on the borderline of legality. With continued illness and a partial disability, the elder Bolan fell behind in his payments . . . and the terror began for the Bolan family. Sam was physically attacked; repeatedly. Young Johnny Bolan was approached by a theft ring, his seventeen-year-old sister by a prostitution ring—with suggestions as to how they could "bail your old man outta trouble."

Johnny Bolan demurred.

Cindy Bolan did not. Her father was suffering a serious heart condition. Continued pressures and violent intimidation would kill him, she felt. Cindy became a "sponsored" prostitute, turning over her earnings toward the discharge of Sam Bolan's indebtedness.

Upon learning of this, the elder Bolan "went berserk." In a frenzy of soul-torment, Sam Bolan shot his daughter, his son, his wife, then turned the gun on himself. Only young Johnny survived to tell the tale, and it was a story to clamp the jaw and ice the eyes of big brother Mack, a combat specialist who had earned the tag "The Executioner" in the jungles and hamlets of Southeast Asia.

"Cindy did only what she thought had to be done. In his own mixed-up way, I guess Pop did the same. Can I do any less?" By this simple declaration was Mack Bolan's "war against the Mafia" enjoined. In the beginning, however, he did not think of it as a war, nor did he even know that the culprits were *Mafiosi*. He knew only that he was performing an act of justice in an area in which the police had already professed helplessness. He "executed" all five officials of the "loan company"—and, hours later, he knew that he had started another "war without end."

"The *Mafia*, for God's sake. So what? They can't be any more dangerous or any smarter than the Cong. Scratch five, and how many are left? A hundred? A thousand? Ten thousand? So— I've got another unwinnable war on my hands."

In a modern army heavy on specialties, Sergeant Bolan had practiced the oldest specialty of all. He was a death specialist. He was an expert marksman in virtually every personal-weapon category. He was a trained sniper, a skilled armorer and an experienced and wily jungle fighter. He was a man who could operate alone and in enemy territory, for long periods, living entirely off the land and by his own wits.

Few men could have been better equipped for the new job which Mack Bolan had taken upon himself. Still, the outcome of his impossible home-front war could have been foretold from the first shot fired. There was no way that a lone man, *any* lone man, could successfully challenge the might and the reach of the most formidable criminal organization ever to arise upon this planet. U.S. government officials called it "the invisible second-government of the nation." Crusading journalists, racket-busting prosecutors and congressional probers alike had repeatedly warned of the enormous tentacles of "this underground monster" which were spreading like cancerous growths throughout the fibre of American life—and yet all had agreed that little could be done within the existing framework of the American system of jurisprudence to effectively combat the power of highly organized crime.

14

So yes, Bolan soon learned what he was going against. He came to know, also, that his enemies could never forgive or forget the challenge to their omnipotence. They quickly felt a necessity to squash him—as an object lesson, if nothing else. An empire built upon terror and violence must sustain itself by those same methods. And even if the Mafia did not get him, the police eventually would. Bolan came to be as guilty of murder and other high crimes as were his opponents, in the eyes of the law. From the moment when that first shot of his home front war was fired, Bolan was a living dead-man and he knew it.

He declared, nevertheless, "I will not roll over and die for them."

What did a condemned man have to lose?

The combat specialist from Vietnam resolved to give meaning to his death. He had lived as a professional soldier; he would die like one. His "last mile" would be a bloody one, and not all of the blood would be his own. He would hit their house with thunder and lightning, he would shake and rattle them while he died, and they would know that there was a price to be paid for their way of life.

So Mack Bolan transplanted his jungle warfare techniques to the city streets of America, where he took the offensive against "this greater enemy."

Much to his own surprise, that initial campaign in his home town, Pittsfield, was a resounding success . . . and surprisingly Bolan lived on while the local house of Mafia virtually disintegrated.

It was a hollow victory, of course. Bolan was now "deader" than ever . . . with a $100,000 bounty on his head, swarms of *Mafiosi* and am-

15

bitious freelancers on his trail, and law enforcement agencies around the nation gearing for his apprehension.

Operating as much on instinct as by the intellect, the young warrior's survival mechanisms directed him into a guerrilla lifestyle. The entire world became his personal jungle of survival, and every chance encounter with another human being became a possible do-or-die situation. To the threatened and the condemned, "aloneness" becomes the heaviest cross to bear. Bolan was not that much different from other men—he sought the comfort and protection of loyal friends—and, shortly after the opening battle in Pittsfield, he turned up on the far side of the country, in Los Angeles, where he hastily recruited his Death Squad of combat buddies from Vietnam.

This maneuver was swiftly revealed as an error in judgment, from Bolan's point of view. The squad was dramatically successful, in that they shattered the powerful DiGeorge family of Southern California—but it was another hollow victory for the Executioner, with seven dead friends on his conscience and the others in police custody. He went on to single-handedly finish off the DiGeorge family, thereafter shunning even the most casual contact with those who might feel inclined to aid him.

A man with Bolan's dedication commanded respect and loyalty, though, whether or not he sought it, and he found many helping hands as his wipe-out trail lengthened and broadened into a seemingly infinite theatre of operations: from the American Southwest to Miami, international forays into France and England, and back through

New York, Chicago, Las Vegas as the ocean of blood around him grew, then a quick dip into the Caribbean area, westward again to San Francisco followed by a searingly urgent call on Boston and a spine-tingling probe of the sub-government scene in Washington.

None knew better than Bolan himself that his survival thus far was due in large part to the efforts of many unsolicited friends in the police establishment, in the general community, and even—here and there—in the Mafia families themselves. He did not discount the value of this assistance; he did wish to keep his personal involvements to an absolute minimum, however, for various reasons.

Howlin' Harlan presented a personal involvement.

San Diego itself would mean a personal involvement, via the personages of Pol Blancanales and Gadgets Schwarz.

The Executioner could not storm that town. The whole community was too tightly interlaced with the rot, knowingly and unknowingly . . . a "cure" could very easily kill the patient, if not undertaken with delicacy.

Bolan had no wish to subject that lovely old town to an indiscriminate washing with hellfire.

So . . . yes . . . any incursion into that complex paradise would have to be done softly and cautiously—in the beginning, anyway.

And he would need the brainy remnants of his old death squad.

Blancanales was an expert at acquiring and organizing military intelligence, at blending like a chameleon into any environment.

Schwarz was an electronics genius who could design and build the most sophisticated surveillance devices from scratch.

Both men also knew how to account for themselves in a firefight.

Howlin' Harlan Winters, though . . . now there was something else. A totally unknown quality in this new war. Friend or enemy? Bolan could not say. The shadows he'd dredged up in Washington were sending up faint little cries from the depths of his mind . . . *careful, careful.* But . . . the Colonel had pinned a couple of decorations on Mack Bolan's chest during that other war . . . and they had faced death together on more than one occasion. What would they be facing in San Diego? Dishonor?

Possibly. Maybe even *national* dishonor.

The man in black shook his head with a perplexed narrowing of his eyes as he gazed out across the lights of the city.

Well, dammit. . . .

Some things a guy simply had to play by ear and heart.

San Diego, then.

Death, dishonor, hell itself . . . come what may . . . San Diego had joined the Executioner's hit parade.

1: PENETRATION

They were Dobermans, a matched set, and the two of them hit the hurricane fence together, each with all four feet scrambling for a hold on the steel mesh, great slavering heads lunging over the top of the barrier, lips curled back in the attack, dripping fangs slashing toward a taste of the man on the outside.

Bolan was damned glad that fence was there.

With a shivering gut, he realized that those sentry dogs fit the rest of the place, and he found himself wondering if there wasn't a better way to begin the probe into San Diego.

The house occupied a sparsely populated stretch of highrise coastline just north of Torrey Pines State Park. It was not a spectacular place—not exactly in the millionaire class—but it seemed to offer the sort of comfort and seclusion which might be sought by a retired combat officer turned industrialist . . . with something or someone to fear.

An English tudor style, it probably combined all the charm of an earlier age with the most lavish conveniences of the late twentieth century—and it was not a bad way for an old soldier to fade away.

As for the super-security—this seemed to fit the new image of General Harlan Winters—the image which had lately become so disquieting to the world's foremost Mafia-fighter.

A row of stubby, wind-stunted trees marked the circular periphery of the cliffside property. Set just inside this natural barrier was a double row of hurricane-fencing spaced about ten feet apart, neither row being of forbidding height but high enough to discourage the casual trespasser.

As a further note, bright red signs were placed along the outer fence with the warnings:

DANGER
GUARD DOG RUN

In this regard, Rosario "Politician" Blancanales had earlier made his scouting report to Bolan: "He keeps a couple of ornery Dobermans penned up in a little demilitarized zone surrounding the house. You don't go through there without permission, unless you want to get eaten alive."

So Bolan had come prepared for the Dobermans.

"Crossman air pistol, hypo darts," he had decided. And he'd instructed Blancanales, "Check the dosage carefully. We just want to put them down for a half-hour or so, not forever."

So now here he was at Howlin' Harlan's Del Mar beach house and it was time for the first probe into the trouble at San Diego. The weather was one of those fantastic Chamber of Commerce specials—a night almost as bright as day with the moon and stars seeming to hover at fingertip distance, the entire area wearing the heavens like a close-fitting bonnet—the breeze coming in off the Pacific like a lover's moist kiss.

Yeah, a night for romance, Bolan thought wryly—not warfare.

But warfare it had to be.

The saliva-dripping snarls from the Dobermans were not exactly moist kisses, and their rebounds against the heavy fencing were becoming frantic under the kill-instinct.

The tall man in combat black cooly checked the load in the Crossman, then he thrust the muzzle through the steel mesh of the fence and sent a syringe through. It caught the nearest dog in the tender zone just inside the shoulder. He sat down quickly, as though someone had thrown a de-activate-switch inside his head, whimpering and licking at the offended zone.

The other one went down just as quickly and peacefully.

Blancanales moved out of the tree cover and bent his back beside the fence. Bolan took the boost and went over quickly. As he touched down inside, the Politician showed him a droll smile and murmured, "I *think* there were just two."

Bolan whispered, "Funny, that's funny," and knelt to examine the tranquilized animals. He withdrew the darts and ruffled the fur in the areas of entry, then passed the Crossman and the darts through to his companion. "Okay, I'll take it from here," he growled. "Get on station and stay hard."

Blancanales tossed an exaggerated salute and abruptly disappeared into the trees. Bolan crossed the dog run and scaled the interior fence, then made a cautious advance across the grounds, blending with the landscape and the shadows wherever possible.

He was in blacksuit. Hands and face were also blackened. At his right hip was the formidable .44 AutoMag—beneath the left arm, the black and silent Beretta. Slit pockets on the lower legs held a variety of small tools. Several miniaturized electronic gadgets were carried in a belly-pouch.

Halfway across the grounds, Bolan paused in the shadow of a flowering shrub to establish contact with the warwagon, left several hundred yards behind under the command of Herman "Gadgets" Schwarz.

"I'm inside," Bolan reported in a husky whisper. "How's it sound?"

A tiny voice purred up from his shoulder in reply: "Great, coming in five-square on all channels. It's a go."

Bolan went.

This was to be a soft probe, an intelligence mission—not a hard hit.

Howlin' Harlan had once been a friend.

The problem now was one of re-identification. Harlan Winters, Brigadier General, U.S. Army retired. Friend or foe?

Either way, Bolan knew, Winters could well be

the most dangerous problem so far encountered in this eternal damned war of his.

He could very well become the final problem.

By all the indicators, Howlie was a high-priced front man for the syndicate. Bolan had known of those indicators even before his arrival in San Diego.

Indicators, of course, were not always accurate.

If the general was *really* in a mess, Bolan could not turn his back on the man.

On the other hand . . . if Howlie was as dirty as Bolan suspected . . . then he could not turn his back on that, either.

Yeah, it could become a twenty-karat mess.

Therefore, friend or foe, the seal on General Winters had to be complete, positive and one hundred percent authentic. And it had to be done without the general's knowledge.

So this was more than a simple soft probe. It was a target-verification mission.

Howlin' Harlan Winters, once one of the most respected strategists in Vietnam, had to be outflanked and sealed.

And, yeah, San Diego was going to be one hell of an interesting war zone.

It had not been a spur of the moment decision to penetrate the Winters place, but a carefully planned operation, entailing several days of patient scouting and fastidious intelligence-gathering.

The job inside the house would require only a few minutes to perform. But only because so much attention had gone into advance preparations.

Bolan had scouted the terrain by boat, by car and on foot—covering specific periods of both day and night—noting comings and goings, visitors, trying to get some feel for the household routine, the people who lived there, worked there, slept there.

Blancanales, meanwhile, had nosed around the area in a home-delivery bakery truck, seeking and cultivating talkative neighbors, tradesmen, and local characters.

Gadgets Schwarz had engineered a telephone tap from the primary cable junction and had 48 hours of electronic surveillance recorded on the gear inside the warwagon.

So, sure, the thing should have gone pretty smooth. Bolan had known exactly where to go and which areas to avoid. He had a diagram of the interior layout of the house—he knew the ins and outs of the place—and he knew how to accomplish the most good in the least time.

The idea had been to rig the joint for sound, all the places that mattered, anyway—the entrance hall, the study, the dining room and a private little secondary study which adjoined the general's bedroom.

And, yeah, it should have gone off like clockwork.

It did not.

Bolan's first stop was at the large combination library-study at the downstairs rear.

Dying embers glowed feebly in a huge rock fireplace.

The only other light was at the far corner of the

room, where a hi-intensity beam lamp was brightly illuminating a small area of a gleaming mahogany desk and offering the stark profile of a lovely young woman who stood woodenly behind the desk.

She was a tall girl, mid-twenties or thereabouts, soft blonde hair lying on golden shoulders, wide spaced eyes with lots of depth which right now seemed to be reflecting hell itself. She was wearing a see-through sleep outfit, and there were many interesting revelations there.

Bolan knew at first glance that she was Lisa Winters, the general's niece. He'd watched her through binoculars earlier that day as she swam and sunned nude on the private beach below the house.

She looked even better in the close-up, despite the fact that she appeared ready to come totally unglued at any moment.

Howlin' Harlan was present, also—in a sense.

His body was slumped in a large wingback chair near the fireplace. Both arms dangled stiffly toward the floor. Part of his skull was missing. A lot of blood had streamed down the face and dried there. Dark stains and splotches across the front of the fireplace showed where more of it had gone.

He'd been dead awhile.

An army Colt .45 lay on the floor beneath his right hand.

The girl was staring at Bolan as though she'd been standing there waiting for him to come in and take charge.

He went straight to the general and dropped to one knee in front of the chair, inspecting without

25

touching the grisly remains of the fightin'est chicken colonel he'd ever served under.

Bolan growled, "Gadgets."

A cautious "Yo," responded via his shoulderphone.

"Howlin' Harlan is dead."

After a brief pause, Schwarz's choked voice replied, "Roger."

"Mission scrubbed. Tell Pol. I'm rejoining."

"Roger."

Bolan sighed to his feet and swiveled about to regard the girl. She had not moved a muscle.

He said, simply, "Too late."

"Long ago," she said. Her throat was dry and the words came out withered and gasping for life.

"What?" Bolan asked, not sure he'd understood.

"It's been too late for a long time," she repeated listlessly. Her eyes raked him from head to toe with half-hearted interest. "What are you, a Del Mar commando or something?"

He replied, "Or something," and turned his back on her to examine the smouldering ashes of the fireplace.

"I burned it all," she told him, the voice rising and bristling with taut defiance. "So you can go back and tell that to whomever sent you."

Bolan muttered, "The hell you did." He was gingerly salvaging a sheaf of scorched and blackened papers.

"That's all you care about, isn't it!" the girl screeched. "The damned papers! They're all any of you care about!"

She was at the edge of hysteria. Bolan went on

about his business, extinguishing the dying sparks and carefully stuffing the salvage into his belly pouch. Then he went to the bar, poured a slug of scotch into a water glass, carried it to the girl, and held it to her lips. She sipped without argument, then strangled and pushed the glass away.

"I don't need that," she gasped.

"When did it happen?" he asked gruffly.

"I don't know. I just—who are you? How'd you get in here?"

"Have you called anyone yet?" Bolan asked, ignoring her queries.

She shook her head.

"It's time to." He picked up the telephone. "Who do you want to call?"

"Carl, I guess."

"Who is Carl?"

"Carl Thompson, our attorney."

Bolan found the number on a phone list attached to the base of the telephone. He set up the call, waited for the first ring, then pressed the instrument into the girl's hand and steered it to her head.

He went away, then, pausing at the doorway long enough to make sure that she had made a connection.

As he faded through the doorway he heard her saying, "Carl, this is Lisa. The general shot himself. He's dead. Help me. God please help. . . ."

Howlin' Harlan Winters had been "sealed" for good.

And, yeah. It was going to be a hell of an interesting war zone.

2: ONE FOR THE MAN

He had been an OD soldier—a cigar chewing, cussing, emotional and one hell of an inspiring C.O.—a true leader whom men followed because he led, not because he'd been created by Act of Congress.

He hadn't always been the most popular officer in camp. Some men found it hard to measure up to Howlin' Harlan's image of the fighting man. They muttered and bitched and frequently promised themselves that they'd shoot him in the back some dark night, and a few openly entertained ideas of shooting themselves as a means of being rotated out of Howlie's command—but one and all respected the man; some openly and warmly loved Harlan Winters; others would have gladly given their lives for his.

He'd been a latter-day Patton, a real soldier's soldier.

Yet, less than a year into civilian clothes, he had died in utter defeat.

This was the part which Mack Bolan could not accept.

Sure, good men sometimes went wrong.

But not that wrong.

Bolan could not buy it. He could not read Harlan Winters as a suicide.

"So what's your reading, then?" Blancanales asked him.

"I don't know," Bolan muttered in reply. "I'm no cop. Even if I were, though, I'd have the same signs to read. The signs all say, sure, Howlie knew the world was closing in on him and he took the easy way out. My gut can't read signs though, Pol. And in my gut I know that all the signs are wrong."

Schwarz put in, "Mine agrees. Howlie didn't kill himself."

The three men had been working for hours over the charred papers which Bolan had salvaged from the Winters' fireplace.

Twelve sheets of typewritten correspondence had been fairly well-reconstructed; these seemed to be an exchange between Winters and a Pentagon official involving "Quality Acceptance Waivers" on several large shipments of war materiel which the Winters firm was producing under government contract.

Various other charred remnants provided intelligence which seemed to confirm the suspicion about Harlan Winters which Bolan had brought from Washington.

A few months after his retirement from active duty, the general had popped up as president of a newly-formed California corporation which was geared entirely to the needs of the military. "Winco" was actually a mini-conglomerate, a merger of a half-dozen or so previously obscure companies which had never been directly engaged in government-contract work. Winco, however, came to life with several sizeable contracts already in its corporate pocket.

The meteoric rise of the new organization, together with a variety of suspicious circumstances, brought it under the scrutiny of several governmental investigative bodies.

Each of the several investigations had been quickly and quietly halted, at the Washington level, mainly through the efforts of a syndicate honcho Bolan had left dead in Washington.

So, sure, Bolan had known a thing or two about his ex-C.O.'s civilian activities, even before San Diego. He had known, also, that one day he might be faced with the unavoidable task of descending *as* the Executioner upon the man who had *created* the Executioner.

Howlin' Harlan had been Bolan's mentor, several life-times ago. The then-lieutenant colonel had been in Vietnam since before the Gulf of Tonkin escalation—first as a military advisor and later as a Green Beret specialist in counter-guerilla warfare.

Bolan had come into the combat theatre as an armor specialist and volunteer advisor in the effort to equip and train the fierce Montagnard tribesmen. Eventually he found himself with a small team of American advisors under the direct command of the already legendary Howlin' Harlan.

In such an operation there was no room for the military formalities which customarily serve as a wall between an officer and his men. Bolan and Winters became a pair, each hugely respecting the professional abilities of the other. The colonel was particularly impressed with Bolan's cool marksmanship and his steely self-command under combat stress.

Under the tutelage and direction of Howlie Winters, Sgt. Bolan became the original "execution specialist" in that theatre of operations. The first Penetration Team was formed around his particular abilities, designed to penetrate and operate deep within enemy-held territory for long periods without direct support of any nature—and Howlin' Harlan himself had gone along on the first few "shakedown cruises" of this potent idea in psychological counterwar. Those early excursions, in fact, had teamed only Winters and Bolan with a five-man support group of specially selected Montagnards.

These were the "proof" runs.

Later, the penetration teams were almost wholly American and they operated wherever enemy occupation and terrorism was present; later still, they were given missions to pursue enemy terrorists into sanctuary areas, though these assignments rarely found their way into the official record.

Howlin' Harlan had not been the sort of man to be bound by legalities. "There are no rules of warfare," he'd often told Bolan. "The only rule of warfare is to *win*."

31

Harlan Winters had grown accustomed to winning, and his "death specialist" teams became known and feared in every enemy camp in Southeast Asia.

PenTeam Able had been the first, though—and that one was Bolan's team.

He had continued to receive the rougher missions. And Howlin' Harlan, now a full chicken colonel in charge of all the teams, often accompanied Able Team on some of the briefer penetrations.

Yes, they'd been a pair.

Together they'd subsisted on jungle roots and swamp grass, insects and wild animals, lying half-submerged in rice paddies or squatting semi-upright in canals and enemy-infested junglelands. Together they'd scouted the Ho Chi Minh trail and mini-blitzed it at carefully selected points from one end to the other; together they'd invaded the terrorist sanctuaries in Laos and Cambodia; together they had many times fought their way back across miles of hostile and aroused territory in hair-raising withdrawals to safe country.

Yeah. Bolan knew the inside of Howlin' Harlan Winters like he knew himself.

And no, hell no, he could not accept this man's death as a weakling's act of self-destruction.

As for the other—the mob involvement—that idea had not been so irreconcilable with the image of the man. Winters had been the type of guy who made his own rules and constructed his own vision of morality. He had continually bucked the "political system" which he blamed for prolonging the war. Often he had ignored official directives and policy decisions from Saigon and Washington.

On more than one occasion Bolan had suspected that his C.O. was falsifying reports on the Pen-Team strikes.

Eventually "the system" had caught up with the maverick colonel. Quietly and with notable absence of ceremonial honors he'd been relieved of his combat command and rotated to a desk job in the Saigon headshed. All his troopers had known, though, that his rotation orders had come from the highest Pentagon sources. "Howlie" had become too much of a colorful personality; war correspondents had latched onto the guy and had, in effect, written him out of the war. The Vietnam thing had become a hot issue in the American press, and Howlin' Harlan Winters represented too much of a potential embarrassment to the men in Washington.

Several months later, Bolan himself had come up for routine rotation. He took a month's leave in the states, then requested reassignment to his old outfit. The request was promptly granted and Bolan returned to the war zone for another full combat tour with the PenTeams. He had never again seen Harlan Winters, however, until that confrontation with sudden and complete retirement in the general's study in Del Mar.

Bolan had not always agreed with everything Harlan Winters stood for. He had not always approved of his C.O.'s official conduct. But he had loved and respected the man for the soldier that he was and now, in San Diego, resolved to give the memory of a valiant warrior a decent burial.

He was fully prepared to acknowledge the almost certain truth that his old commander had been knowingly involved with the Mafia.

33

There were indications, even, that this involvement extended back into the general's GHQ stint at Saigon, during the post-combative period.

But he was not ready yet to bury Harlan Winters without military honors.

"So where do we go from here?" Blancanales wanted to know.

Bolan quietly replied, "We go into enemy territory, Pol. Into the sanctuaries. We go in there and drag the colonel out. Okay?"

The other two veterans of Able Team exchanged glances, then Gadgets Schwarz cleared his throat and said, "Right. It's a rescue mission."

"For a dead man," Blancanales sighed.

"For the memory of a good soldier," Bolan corrected him. "Howlin' Harlan deserves an Able Team effort. Right?"

"Right," Schwarz echoed.

"But no false reports," Blancanales said quietly.

"We just bring him out," Bolan agreed. "The man that was there can speak for himself."

"Agreed," Blancanales replied. "We'll give it one good rattle for the man."

The tentative siege of San Diego had not been lifted.

On the contrary, it had suddenly undergone massive intensification.

Able Team was on the job.

3: ON NOTICE

The first gray fingers of dawn were pushing into the cloudless Southern California sky and darkly silhouetting the rugged rise of mountain peaks to the north and east.

Montgomery Field, a suburban airport favored by private and charter pilots, lay quietly brooding upon the approaching daylight.

Several men in white coveralls, employees of the flying service which operated the airport facilities, moved slowly among the small craft in the tie-down area in a routine inspection.

Runway lights and the field beacon were still in operation, and brightness spilled from several open hangars.

From the base operator's private terminal could be heard the clacking of a flight-advisory teletype.

Manuel "Chicano" Ramirez and Jack "Schoolteacher" Fizzi occupied a late-model LTD, parked near a service ramp in the shadows of the terminal building. The windows were down and Fizzi was lightly drumming his fingers on the roof of the vehicle, keeping time with a country-music tune from the car radio.

Ramirez, the wheelman, a heavy man with a lumpy face and shaggy hair—expensively attired but rumpled and obviously disrespectful of $200 suits. He was about forty and well known in the police files of several nations. At the moment, the Chicano was slumped behind the wheel of the car, eyes closed, seemingly dozing.

Fizzi was in his late twenties. He had attended a small eastern college for two years, then traveled west to seek his fortune. One year to the day after his arrival in California, Fizzi began a one-to-five tenure at Folsom Prison for Grand Theft—Auto. For the next twenty months he had worked in the prison's rehabilitation program as a teacher of illiterate cons. Apparently he had learned more than he taught at Folsom. His "connection" with Ben Lucasi, overlord of Southern California organized crime, was arranged within a few weeks of his release from confinement.

The Schoolteacher was always sharply dressed, almost tensely alert, his hair longish but carefully groomed in the new mod look. The image projected was the new look in junior executive. It was a false image.

The big man behind the wheel lifted his head sluggishly from the back rest and growled, "Wha' time is it?"

"Time enough," Fizzi replied. "He's ten minutes late."

"Hate these fuckin' milk runs," the other complained.

"Me too." The handsome one sighed, adding, "This will be the last for awhile." He turned off the radio. "Maybe they hit some bad weather."

"Go ask the guy inside," Ramirez suggested.

"Aw no. He'll be here."

Two men wearing the white coveralls of the flying service rounded the corner of the terminal building and approached the vehicle.

"Ask these grease monkeys."

"What the hell do they know?" Fizzi growled. "He's been late before. Just cool it."

The men in white were making a casual approach, laughing softly between themselves until reaching the LTD, then they split and came down opposite sides of the car.

The one moving along the driver's side was about medium height, somewhat thickset, dark hair and skin, smile-wrinkles setting the expression of the face.

The man at the other side was tall, broad-shouldered, athletically built—a bit younger than his companion—with chiseled features and eyes that dominated the entire appearance.

"Ask 'em," the wheelman insisted.

Fizzi growled a profanity and thrust his head outside just as the tall man drew abreast. "Hey, jock, what's the weather report for the mountains?" he asked in a snarly monotone.

"Stormy," the big guy replied in a voice of sheerest ice. A silencer-tipped black auto appeared in his hand from seemingly nowhere, to graft itself to Fizzi's outthrust forehead.

A gasp from the other side of the car signalled

that the same unsettling event had occurred over there. The young triggerman very carefully relaxed his tightening muscles and his tone was entirely respectful as he said, "Okay, all right, okay. Let's cool it. What's the beef?"

The tall man issued another quiet single-word response: "Outside."

It was like a voice from some deepfreeze, not calculated to encourage inane argument.

The guy backed off, just a little, the ominous tip of that black pistol unwaveringly remaining on target though, his free hand opening the door and swinging it wide.

Fizzi slid carefully to the outside, keeping his hands in clear view. As though acting out a conditioned reflex, he then turned his back on the big guy, spread his feet, raised his hands, and fell forward against the roof of the car in a "frisk" stance.

Somewhat the same scene was being enacted at the opposite side of the vehicle.

Ramirez was growling, "Where's your warrant? I wanna see a warrant."

"What're you guys—feds?" Fizzi wanted to know as the tall man relieved him of his weapon.

That same icy voice replied, "Sort of."

Before he quite realized that it was happening, Fizzi then found that his wrists were securely taped together at his back and the guy was applying a wide strip of adhesive to his mouth. An instant later he and Ramirez were curled into the trunk compartment and the guy was shoving something into his fist—something small and metallic with irregular edges.

Then the trunk lid was closed and he was sharing the cramped darkness with Ramirez.

He maneuvered the little metallic object into his palm and rubbed his fingers along the outline —and suddenly Fizzi knew what that object was.

He also knew who the big bastard was.

And he knew, with a flooding sense of relief, that he was one lucky goddam triggerman if he was really going to get off this easy.

Not many guys ever met Mack Bolan and lived to brag about it.

Yeah. Jack the Schoolteacher was one goddam lucky son of a bitch.

But why? for God's sake *why* had the guy left him breathing?

A sharp little red and white Cessna came in just ahead of the sunrise to execute a standard landing approach in the Montgomery Field traffic pattern. It touched down smoothly on the main runway, completed a short landing roll and crossed over to the service area, halting at the gas pumps just uprange from the waiting automobile.

One Sammy Simonetti, the lone passenger, stepped outside, then leaned in for a final instruction to the pilot. "After you've gassed up, put her away. We won't be going back until tonight late."

The pilot nodded. "You'll know where to find me."

"Right."

Simonetti was a "courier." He even looked like one, complete to the wrist-manacle attache case which was chained to his right hand.

Two men in airport service-white moved out

39

of the lengthening shadows of the terminal building and intercepted him halfway between plane and car.

"Mr. Simonetti?" the thickset one pleasantly greeted him.

The messenger frowned, but broke stride and replied, "Yeah?"—his eyes flicking toward the waiting vehicle.

The tall man quietly informed him, "Trip ends right here, Sammy."

The ominously-tipped black Beretta showed itself, the muzzle staring up into the courier's eyes.

The other man reached inside of Simonetti's jacket, took his weapon, then nudged him on toward the LTD.

"You guys out of your minds or something?" he asked them in a choked voice. "You know who you're hitting?"

"We know," the tall one assured him. He opened a rear door and shoved the flustered man into the back seat.

The other guy was sliding in from the opposite doorway. He grabbed Simonetti's hand and went to work on the wrist-lock with a small tool.

The captive's eyes were showing panic. He groaned, "Hey, Jesus, don't do this to me. How'm I going to tell Mr. Lucasi about this? I can't go walking in there with a naked arm."

"You'll think of something," the pleasant one replied.

"Look, boys, no shit now. You want to make a score? I mean a *real* score? Look, leave it alone. There's nothing in here to do you any good. I can steer you to a *real* score. I mean, millions maybe."

The icy one commanded, "Shut up, Sammy."

40

"Look, you're never going to be able to enjoy it. You know what I mean. You can't just walk up and hit the combination this way. You're dead men the minute you walk away from here. Get smart, hell man. I can steer you—"

The Beretta's silencer had steered itself right into Sammy Simonetti's hardworking mouth. He froze, then made a pleading sound around the new pacifier.

The big guy gave him a moment to get the feel and taste of oral death, then he withdrew the weapon and told the shaken courier, "Not another word."

Simonetti's eyes promised total silence and a moment later the other guy defeated the lock at his wrist.

The guy chuckled and told him, "Count your blessings, buddy. I was about ready to take arm and all."

The hard one placed the car keys in the courier's freed hand and told him, "Look in the trunk. But not right away. You wait awhile."

Simonetti nodded his head in thoroughly cowed silence and the two men in white turned their backs on him and walked around the building and out of sight.

He'd been on the ground less than a minute.

Who would ever believe this?

That slick and that easy, those guys had just clipped the combination for more than a hundred grand.

Nobody would believe that . . . especially not Ben Lucasi!

The shaken messenger rattled the car keys in

his hand, wondering vaguely what the guy had meant by, "Look in the trunk."

What would he find in there? The remains of Chicano and the Schoolteacher?

Simonetti shivered.

Nobody would believe this.

Then he became aware that something was mixed in with the keys in his hand—he'd thought it to be part of the keyring or something.

But it was definitely not a part of the key ring.

They didn't put marksman's medals on key rings.

A chill ran the entire length of Simonetti's spine and his guts began to quake.

Jesus!

They'd believe it, all right.

Goddammed right they'd believe it!

4: THE TRACK

The San Diego territory had long been considered a tenderloin area for *La Cosa Nostra*. This "key" territory—bounded on one side by one of the world's ten greatest natural harbors and on another by the Mexican border—until recently had functioned as an "arm" of the DiGeorge Family, the Los Angeles mob which had already tasted the Executioner's war effort.

With DiGeorge's death and the dissolution of that "family," the national ruling council, *La Commissione*, stepped in to administer the syndicate's interests in that area.

Ben Lucasi had been a DiGeorge underboss. He and "Deej" had been longtime friends. He'd hated to see Deej have to go that way . . . but in his secret moments, Lucasi would admit that even the darkest cloud usually carried a silver lining.

Under the new setup, Big Ben was practically autonomous—reporting directly to the Commission of Capo's at the national level of government.

San Diego was no longer an "arm" of anything or anybody. San Diego now belonged to Big Ben Lucasi, period. And, yeah, Big Ben (who measured 5'4" even in elevator shoes and weighed-in soaking wet at 120 pounds) liked things a hell of a lot better that way.

He was not, of course, a full-fledged *Capo*. Not yet. But that honor would come, just like all the other good things had come. The whole California territory was reorganizing itself around San Diego.

One of these days the boys all around the country would be referring to this arm as *The Lucasi Family*. And why not? Where the money was, that's where the power was—and now that he was no longer getting a lot of jealous bullshit from L.A., Ben Lucasi was mining the San Diego gold like it hadn't been mined since the forty-niners.

What with *Agua Caliente* a few minutes south and with Las Vegas just a hop over the mountains by plane—hell, a guy would have to have his mind in his balls not to make a goldmine out of that happy circumstance. And the whole goddam fuckin' U.S. Navy sitting out here at his right hand, running back and forth to the Orient—what kind of a lamebrain wouldn't turn a thing like that to his profit?

Some of the locals were starting to snicker about his "seagoing Mafia." Which was okay. Let them make jokes. Lucasi owned also a "khaki Mafia." Let 'em laugh—that was okay. As long as everybody was laughing there'd be no worry. Meanwhile San Diego was fast becoming the underground capital of the western world, and Ben Lucasi was becoming the most powerful non-*Capo* anywhere.

The Lucasi home was an unpretentious but modern split-level situated in one of the new neighborhoods near Mission Bay Park. He lived there with his third wife, Dorothy—a 23-year-old ex-showgirl from Las Vegas. Lucasi was 56. He had a daughter, 35, and a son, 32, from his first marriage. The son worked in a casino in Nassau; the daughter, at last report, was somewhere in Europe "with another lousy gigolo."

The first Mrs. Lucasi had died under mysterious circumstances while the children were still quite young, during that era when Bennie was scrambling everywhere for the buck. His criminal record from those early days reveals arrests for pandering, rape, felonious assault, theft, gambling, arson, extortion, intimidation, black-marketeering, manslaughter, and murder. The official FBI report on this very busy criminal enumerated 52 specific charges . . . with but 2 convictions and 2 suspended sentences.

He had spent a combined total of 66 days behind bars.

His last arrest had occurred in 1944, on a black-marketing charge.

Lucasi had come west at the end of the war, settling first in Reno, Nevada for a few years, then on to Las Vegas when the boom began there. In the late fifties he relocated to San Francisco, later gravitating to Los Angeles for a lieutenancy under Julian DiGeorge, who eventually sent him on to San Diego to boss that arm of the family.

So, sure. Except for a few nervous moments here and there, the world was looking rosy indeed for this late-blooming syndicate boss. The nervous moments came from increased anti-crime activity at the federal level—the damned Strike Forces— and a growing awareness among local citizens regarding the interconnections between the straight and the kinky communities.

And, of course, there was that Bolan bastard.

Bolan had almost torn things for good when he went on the warpath against Deej. The repercussions from that conflict had been felt clear down into San Diego . . . and to points beyond. Lucasi himself had been enroute to Palm Springs when Bolan finally lowered the boom on DiGeorge there. And he'd seen, at first hand, the aftermath of a Mack Bolan hit. Yeah, he still had nightmares sometimes over what he'd seen at Palm Springs.

Goddamn how relieved Bennie had been when Bolan started churning up the turf back east.

Lucasi had thought he was rid of the bastard.

The son of a bitch had been everywhere. He'd hit Miami. He'd hit, for Christ's sake, even over in France and England—and for damn sure Bennie had thought the guy would *stay* over there somewhere and lay low.

Like hell he did. He hit the five family area, New York, like some crazy avenging angel, and just tore the living shit out of that place. *All five families!*

Ben had thought, then, well okay. Go ahead, you crazy bastard. Keep living like that and you won't survive to head west again.

46

Lucasi had been wrong about that, too.

He'd almost prayed that the guy would try Chicago. Yeah, hit Chi now . . . try your luck on a *real* town.

And the son of a bitch did it. And the "real town" folded just like all the others.

Lucasi had begun to feel that this Bolan had some sort of special decree from God or something. No guy—not *no* guy who is one hundred percent mortal—could get away with that kind of shit forever.

So then the guy went into Lucasi's old home base, the town the whole mob loved—Vegas—and Christ, what monkeys he'd made of them all in Vegas.

So, sure. There had to be something eerie about the guy.

Worst of all, the big bastard in Executioner black was west again . . . and Lucasi doubled his palace guard and went nowhere without a heavy escort of bodyguards.

Then the guy bobs up down in Puerto Rico . . . of all the damned places . . . but before Lucasi could start breathing naturally again, there the bastard was up in Frisco and tearing hell out of California again.

It was too much.

Lucasi took a quick vacation to Honolulu.

When he returned, Bolan was back east again, romping through Boston first and then tearing through Washington.

No guy should get away with that much.

No one hundred percent *mortal*.

If somebody didn't stop him pretty soon, he'd be chewing up San Diego one of these days.

And, sure, Bennie Lucasi had a lot of nervous moments.

How did you stop someone like that?

Lucasi had taken to reading up on black magic, ESP, mind control . . . all that. He dipped briefly into Yoga—trying to find Bolan's secret.

He even went to confession at that little mission down on the coast.

The poor hayseed priest had thought Lucasi was bullshitting him. Bawled him out good for playing games with the confession box.

Lucasi lit a candle at that mission, just the same.

That cock Bolan would be trying San Diego sooner or later . . . no doubt about that.

Lucasi had to be ready for him. He had to—somewhere, somehow—find the edge that would equalize Bolan.

He'd been trying. God, he'd tried everything.

And now it seemed that his preparation time had run out.

Sammy Simonetti was standing right there in his living room and handing him the most feared symbol which Ben Lucasi ever expected to see.

A fuckin' marksman's medal.

In a strangely quiet voice, he asked Sammy, "You bringing me this instead of my hundred thou?"

Simonetti was sweating, overly-defensive. "I swear to hell, Mr. Lucasi, the guy just—"

"Where'd you say he hit you?" the chieftain interrupted in that same deadened voice. "Vegas?"

"No sir, right out here on this end, at the airport."

"Where the hell is my black milk, Sammy?"

"Jesus, I told you. *He* took it."

"You still got both arms, I see."

"Yessir, they didn't hardly put a mark on me. That's what I can't understand. They didn't hurt Chicano and Schoolteacher either. Just locked 'em in the trunk of the car."

"They who?" Lucasi muttered.

"Bolan and his triggerman."

"Bolan don't use no triggermen," Lucasi said quickly, a hint of fire returning to his voice.

"He did this time. There were two of them. Come up on me just like a couple of goddamn shadows. I didn't know from nothing, boss. Just all of a sudden here was this damn Beretta looking down my throat."

"The guy works *alone*, you dumb shit!" Lucasi shouted. "Now you get your story straight!"

"Jesus, I swear, it happened just like I said," Simonetti moaned.

Lucasi turned his back on the courier and, to no one in particular, commanded, "Take Sammy outside and get his story straight."

A large man who had been lurking near the door opened it and gave the nod to Simonetti. "Let's go," he growled.

The black-money courier's eyes rolled; he started to give an emotional protest to the boss, then quickly changed his mind and stumbled out the door. Another man fell in behind him, solemnly pulling the door closed behind their exit.

Lucasi was flipping the marksman's medal like a coin, staring past it unseeingly, his eyes characteristically locked into a dead focus while his mind whirred.

Presently he said, quietly, "Somebody could be shooting us full of juice, Diver."

The large man at the door, Lucasi's house captain, replied, "Could be. I been wondering when somebody would try something like that. Those marksman's medals can be picked up most anywhere."

"It doesn't sound like a Bolan hit," Lucasi said.

"No, it don't, Ben."

"You were back east last month. How many of the boys did you run into?"

The large man shrugged. "I guess a dozen or two. Why?"

"New York boys?"

The man nodded. "Yeah. Them too."

"Did you talk to one—just *one*—who'd ever seen Bolan face to face?"

The big man just grinned.

"Of course you didn't," Lucasi said, smirking. "The only boys who've seen Bolan, you'd have to go to hell to talk to them. Right?"

The house captain jerked his head in agreement. "He don't fuck around much, the way I hear it. He just hits and splits, and when he's gone, there ain't nobody around to tell what happened."

"Exactly." Lucasi tossed the medal again and deliberately let it fall to the floor. "So who's got my goddamn hundred thou, Diver?"

"It sounds fishy, all right," the captain agreed. "You go out and help talk to Sammy."

The large man grinned sourly and went out.

Lucasi lit a cigar and worked furiously at it until the tip was glowing fiercely, then he walked stiffly out of the room, along a short hallway to his sleeping quarters.

He went directly to the bed and whipped the covers away from the nude woman who was sleeping there. He yelled, "Outta that rack, you lazy bitch!"

Dorothy Lucasi sleepily sat up, swinging the long Vegas-showgirl legs over the side of the bed. "Are you crazy, Bennie?" she inquired in a practiced monotone. She often asked him that, in the same tone of voice.

His wife stood a full head taller than Lucasi. He glowered at her as she lurched to her feet and looked about dazedly for her dressing gown. Instead of helping her find the wrap, he yelled, "Yeah, I'm crazy to have married a floozy like you!" Lucasi often said that, also.

"You get some clothes on that million dollar meat and hustle it into the kitchen. It's seven o'clock and I goddammit want something to eat!"

She was sleepily complaining, "Why can't Frenchy fix .. ?" when her chin dropped and the words quit coming.

Lucasi thought at first that she was looking at him in some new way he'd never yet seen, then he knew that her transfixed gaze was going beyond him and onto something behind him.

A chill seized his spine and shook it, and he turned slowly to find the object of his wife's rarely undiluted attention.

A big tall guy was just standing there against the wall, next to the window—and he must have been there all the while. He was dressed all in black, with guns and belts and things strapped all over him, and that face was like carved out of Mount Rushmore, except for the peculiarly hot-icy eyes that smouldered out of that deepfreeze.

51

Yeah.

Bolan had come to town, all right.

Lucasi felt himself crumbling inside.

His voice sounded high and squeaky to himself as he told the impressive apparition in black, "So. Sammy had it straight."

The guy wasn't even holding a gun on him . . . the wise cock. He was just standing there, sort of relaxed, staring a hole through Ben Lucasi.

The seconds ticked away, silently. Dorothy sat back down on the bed and modestly covered her lap with a sheet. It was the first act of modesty on her part that Ben Lucasi had ever been aware of. He found himself wondering about the effect this guy had on the dames.

Presently Lucasi cleared his throat and said, "Uh, what do you want, eh?"

"Harlan Winters," the guy replied, and it was a voice straight out of hell.

"Who?" the Mafia chieftain nervously inquired.

Dorothy giggled, like some nut. "Harlie Winters," she said, very helpfully.

"He ain't here," Lucasi declared quickly, wishing he could bust that broad right in the nose.

"He's dead," the big guy said.

Lucasi whispered, "God I'm sorry, I didn't know that."

"Friend of yours?"

The guy sure didn't use many words.

"Uh, well . . . in a way. We, uh . . . met once or twice." He snapped a quick glance toward his wife. She was wearing a shocked face. He hoped to God she'd keep her flannel mouth shut and he kept right on talking to edge her out, just in case. "Winters

52

was a nice man, God—that's terrible. How'd he die?"

"The hard way," the cold voice intoned. "Scattered all over his study."

Lucasi shivered. What kind of cat and mouse game was this? Why God why had he sent Diver and the other boys outside to ask dumb questions of poor Sammy?

So, he had to stall the guy as long as possible, that was the only thing left. God, he didn't even have a gun in here.

He took a deep breath and said, "Look, I don't know why you're coming telling me this. Uh . . . you're Bolan, right? I knew that, I knew it right away. Look man, you're barking up a hollow tree this time. I got no beef with you at all, nothing. So you knocked over one of my messengers, okay. Hell with it, *easy come easy go*, that's the way I look at it. I mean, I got no beef. So you hit this Harlan Winters, okay, like I said, I met 'im once or twice, no big deal. No beef. Now, way I see it. . . ."

Bolan said, "Save your breath." The cold gaze flicked to a watch at his wrist. "You've got twenty seconds."

"For *what?*" Lucasi cried.

"I'm looking for tracks, Bennie."

"What kind of tracks?"

"Who wanted Winters dead?"

"What? You mean you didn't . . . ?"

"I didn't," the icy bastard clipped back. "Who did?"

Lucasi passed a shaking hand over his face. He sighed. Then he said, "Hell, I can't imagine. Why don't you ask Thornton. Maxwell Thornton, the big shot. Yeah. Ask him."

53

Bolan assured him, "I will." Another quick glance at the wristwatch, then, "You and the lady get out of here. Close the door behind you."

"You mean that's ... ?"

"Yeah, that's all for now." Something that might have been a smile flickered across those cold features. "Be seeing you, Bennie."

Lucasi muttered, "Yeah," in a choked voice as he grabbed Dorothy and shoved her out the door. He followed quickly and pulled the door firmly shut, then he left her standing there stupid naked in the hallway and ran shouting into the main part of the house.

Then he saw them through the sliding glass doors to the patio—all his boys—with their tails on the cement and their hands clasped atop their heads.

A couple other guys, dressed just like Bolan, were just then disappearing over the wall . . . and Ben Lucasi knew that he had been very neatly had all the way.

The son of a bitch had just walked in and taken over!

And for what?

For what tracks?

His goddamn khaki Mafia, for God's sake!

But *what tracks?*

5: THE MISSION

They had departed the Lucasi neighborhood on diverging routes and regrouped ten minutes later on a bluff overlooking Mission Bay Park, the city's most popular water playground.

Blancanales still drove the bread truck he'd used in scouting the Winters home. Schwarz had converted Bolan's "warwagon," a Ford Econoline van, into a mobile electronics workshop—and this remained as his base of operations.

Bolan himself was driving a "hot scout"—a speedy, highly-maneuverable, European sports car.

This was their first chance to regroup and report since the hit on Sammy Simonetti at the airport. Each man dismounted from his vehicle and they held a council of war beside Bolan's roadrunner while they pulled concealing coveralls over their combat outfits.

"Sammy's bread is in the bread truck," Blancanales reported, grinning. "It counts out to exactly a hundred and five thousand. What do I do with it?"

"Keep it for the warchest," Bolan replied. "That's one of your problems for this operation. Anything Gadgets and I need, we'll come to you. You make all the buys. Less chancey that way."

Blancanales nodded. "Okay. How'd it go in Lucasi's palace?"

"Damn near disastrous," Bolan said. "The little man walked in while I was sounding his bedroom. You guys did a neat job outside, thanks. Probably saved the day."

"Did you get the bedroom bug planted?" Schwarz wondered.

"Yeah." The man from blood smiled. "In the headboard of his bed, while his wife slept. He's married to a kid . . . but oh, what a kid!"

Blancanales snickered. "Maybe we could sell the tapes to an underground movie outfit."

Schwarz, all business, wanted to know, "Where'd you put the relay stations?"

"Window ledges, outside," Bolan reported. "All aligned at one-five-zero magnetic, per your instructions."

"Then we should have him snockered," Schwarz said. The gadgets-genius glanced at his watch and jotted a note in his surveillance log. "I'll have to cruise by and drain those storage banks in four hours. That's maximum storage, sorry."

Bolan had to grin. It was typical of Gadgets Schwarz to be "sorry" that he could not improve

56

upon perfection. The little devices which he'd designed and built for this job were just about the ultimate in electronics surveillance, to Bolan's mind.

The pickup unit, consisting of a mike and a miniature radio transmitter, was about the size of a lady's wristwatch. The life in the tiny power cell was sufficient to provide 72 hours of continuous operation.

The "relay station," somewhat bulkier but still small enough for easy concealment, received and recorded the continuous broadcast from the pickup unit.

Upon command, the transmitter in the relay station would "unreel" the entire recording disc in about sixty seconds. That command would come from Schwarz's mobile console in the warwagon; he could cruise casually past the house once each four hours and "collect" the intelligence stored in the relay station . . . four hours of electronic surveillance compressed into a sixty-second transmission keyed from the warwagon.

The re-recording, appropriately slowed and automatically performed within the master console, screened out all the silent zones or "lapses" in the four-hour recording, preserving only the "audibles" for fast monitoring in the re-play.

And Gadgets was "sorry" about that.

They had followed Sammy Simonetti from the airport and used the courier's unhappy arrival at the Lucasi household as a diversion for their own penetration.

While Lucasi and his palace guard focused on the implications of Simonetti's busted play, Able

Team slipped quietly in and wired the whole joint for sound.

"You've got four relays plus the phone tap," Bolan reminded Schwarz. "Can you collect them all on one pass?"

"No," Schwarz told him. "I could probably squeeze in two per pass but I'd rather not. A hundred yards is about the maximum reliable range for those relays. That gives me a hundred coming and a hundred going away, strict line-of-sight. I read that as one collection per pass, unless I just pull up and park."

"Pull up and park, then," Bolan suggested. "Change a tire, fiddle with your engine—anything that will cover. But I don't like five times past that house in the same vehicle."

"Okay, I'll park and drain," Schwarz agreed.

"Pol, you stay on Lucasi. Keep a log on his every move outside that house."

"You'll have it," Blancanales quietly replied.

"Did you get those zoom lenses for the camera?"

The Politician nodded his head in reply. "I could probably get a flea from a block away."

"Great. Try to get a picture of every one entering that house, plus every one he meets away from the house. Unless you're really tied into something fantastic, we meet back here in exactly four hours."

"What do I do in the meantime?" Gadgets wondered. "So far I've got a five minute job."

"Run over and drain the phone tap at Howlin' Harlan's," Bolan instructed him. "If you pick up something useful there, don't save it. Beep me on Able Channel."

"Okay. Where will you be?"

"I think I'll be at the Mission Bay marina."

"Who do we know there?" Politician asked.

Bolan smiled. "I hear that Tony Danger keeps a deep-water boat berthed there."

"I guess I never heard of Tony Danger," the Politician murmured.

"One of Lucasi's lieutenants," Bolan explained. "Narcotics, mainly."

"That's the guy," Schwarz commented, "was supposed to get the hundred grand."

"That's him," Bolan confirmed. "I believe he was setting up for a buy. Heroin or cocaine, probably. They usually time the black money shipments for a fast in and out. And I saw Tony Danger at Lucasi's awhile ago, pacing around and wringing his hands over the loss of that shipment. He was wearing a yachting cap."

Blancanales chuckled. "That was Tony Danger, eh?"

"That was him."

"He turned green when I laid that autopistol on him."

"When he's got it all together he can be pretty mean," Bolan warned. "He was one of DiGeorge's favorite triggermen."

Schwarz was wearing a faint frown. He asked, "How does all this tie into the colonel?"

"Maybe not at all," Bolan replied. "I'm just hoping to stir the pot a bit. No telling what might float up off the bottom."

Blancanales suggested, "Maybe some very straight big daddy with a dirty backside."

Bolan nodded. "That's what I'm hoping for. A hell of a lot of mob money is moving into the legit pipelines in this town. That's what put Winco in business . . . black money. But it didn't move directly from Lucasi to Winters. There's a middleman somewhere, a guy with plenty of clout. If we're going to find Howlin' Harlan's lost soul, then we've first got to find the Big Middle."

"Okay, I guess that makes sense," Schwarz said.

"The same guy is providing the umbrella for Lucasi and his hoods," Blancanales added.

"Probably," Bolan said. "It takes a certain kind of environment to support a Mafia entrenchment. If you find that entrenchment, then you know the environment is there also. So we'll try to knock some holes in the entrenchment. Maybe we'll get a glimpse of the environment as it rushes in to plug the holes."

"This is different than the L.A. operation," Schwarz decided.

"Quite a bit," Bolan agreed. "L.A. is a big roaring city, liberal, free-wheeling. That's enough natural environment right there to cover routine mob operations. This is a different sort of environment. Much smaller. Conservative, strong civic spirit, a proud town. Somebody in a position of power and trust within that establishment has to be dirty if the mob is operating here on the scale I suspect."

"Or maybe a bunch of somebodies," Blancanales growled.

"Maybe. Whoever or how many, we have to shake them up, get them churning, worrying. We already have a possible." Bolan stared for a moment at Schwarz. "After you've collected the Winters' intelligence, if you have time, find out what you can about a local wheel named Maxwell Thornton."

"Pretty big guy?" Blancanales inquired.

Bolan replied, "Yeah, pretty big. Let's examine our problem here for a minute. We know the mob people in this area. We know pretty well where their interests lie and the type of routine operations they're running. We could blitz them . . . just lay all over them . . . and we could do that very well, I think. But that wouldn't put us any closer to the deeper enemy, and that is the one we really want this time. The Big Middle . . . that's our target. First, though, we have to find them."

"And you think this guy Thornton may be one of this Big Middle?"

"As I said, he's a possible. Lucasi dropped the name on me. Maybe just as a stall, but sometimes a lot of truth seeps out of a deathbed stall. We have to check it out . . . but very carefully. We don't want to get these guys to running . . . just shaking a little."

Schwarz asked, "What if they won't shake?"

Bolan's voice dropped an octave in the reply. "Then we'll have to burn them out."

The Politician wriggled under an involuntary shiver. He coughed into his fist and said, "I'm starting to understand why you didn't want this town on your hit parade, Sarge. It could get pretty nasty, couldn't it."

Bolan was staring at the tips of his fingers.

Schwarz commented, "What happened to the good old days of simple warfare, eh?"

"They were left quite a ways down the trail," Bolan replied quietly. "The thing gets more complicated all the time, Gadgets."

The expression in the electronics man's eyes reflected a new understanding of this quiet man in executioner black. This was a new Bolan, a wary and sophisticated warrior—essentially the same man he'd known earlier in the wars, but with that subtle shade of difference . . . he was a man with a high mission.

"There'll still be plenty of fireworks before we close this one," Schwarz muttered.

"Bet on it," Blancanales growled. He sighed. "Well, I'd better be moving out. How much range we got on these shoulder phones?"

"Figure ten miles," Schwarz replied thoughtfully, his mind obviously on some other matter.

"Figure a lifetime," Bolan quietly corrected him.

In this business, Bolan knew, each beat of the heart was a lifetime in its own right.

"You guys be very careful," he commanded gruffly. "Play it to the numbers, and very close."

The three solemnly shook hands and went their separate ways.

A city under quiet siege awaited their heartbeats.

6: HARDCASE REVISITED

The daytime routine was barely underway at the Los Angeles Hall of Justice when Captain Tim Braddock found himself in an interesting telephone conversation with his counterpart at San Diego.

"What makes you think you've got Bolan down there?" he asked John Tatum, homicide chief at the southern city.

"It's just an uneasy feeling, at this point," Tatum replied in a troubled voice. "I've never had so much as a smell of the guy before, though . . . I guess I'm hoping you can tell me I'm all wet."

"Well. . . ." Braddock sighed. He and Tatum had been friends for many years. "What've you got, John?"

"Item One, an apparent suicide. Let's talk about that one first. Last night, late. Retired army general, once got a lot of press for his colorful combat activities in Vietnam. Lately head of Winco Industries."

"Howlin' Harlan Winters," Braddock said with a heavy voice.

"You knew him?"

"Not personally. Go on."

"He put an army Colt to his head and pulled the trigger, or so the evidence would indicate. Paraffin tests are positive—all the routine checks and physical evidence support the suicide angle. Coroner agrees."

"Did he leave a note?"

"No note. The county is ready to close it as a suicide, but. . . ."

Braddock lit a cigarette and sucked in a lungful of smoke, exhaled violently and asked, "But?"

"Well . . . Winters was a bachelor. Lived alone, except for a niece. She discovered the body, and—"

"How do you figure Bolan in this? What's your Item Two?"

"I'll take the last question first, it's easier. Somebody pulled a heist on a shipment of cash skimmed from a Vegas casino. Happened just a few hours after Winters died. One of our undercover men phoned in the report a couple hours ago. He says that Ben Lucasi is frothing at the mouth and importing triggermen from all over. Our operative couldn't get the full story, but he says it smells of a Bolan hit."

"Yeah, he likes to hit them in their money bags," Braddock mused. "That's all you have on that?"

"That's it."

"Okay, back to Item One. You think Winters

was murdered, I take it. Is the niece a suspect?"

"Hell *no*, but Bolan is."

Braddock sighed. "Okay, let's have it."

"Let me background you a bit first. Winters had this beach-pad out near Del Mar. You know that area. Fifty percent of his property line fronts on a sheer cliff overlooking the ocean. The only way up from the beach is via an elevator which is controlled from above. In other words, no visitors from below without an invitation from above."

"I have the picture," Braddock said. "But isn't Del Mar out of your jurisdiction?"

"Technically, sure. But we got called in for routine consultation and . . . well . . . look, Tim, if Bolan is operating anywhere between Tijuana and L.A., don't talk to me about police jurisdictions."

Braddock chuckled drily and said, "Well said, John. And welcome to the club."

The San Diego cop was becoming flustered. He growled, "Let me lay this out for you, will you? Now look, half the Winters property is secure from trespassers by the cliff. Okay. The other half is double-fenced and a pair of Doberman maneaters roam a no-man's-land between those fencerows. Those guys are mean as hell—a couple of very unhappy sheriff's deputies will attest to that—and there simply is no way past them without calling the house and getting an escort through the fang zone."

"Okay, this is getting interesting," Braddock commented.

"Yeah. Just wait. Miss Winters says that there were no callers last night. That is, no visitors. She doubles as a girl-Friday, housekeeper, chief-bottle-washer and all the rest for the general. She—"

"How much rest?" Braddock wanted to know.

"What? Oh, nothing like that, Tim. It was more like a father-daughter relationship. Winters raised the girl. Parents died when she was a tot. Army brat. He dragged her around the world with him. I checked her out thoroughly. She's clean."

"Okay. Go on. What about Bolan?"

"Where was I? Okay, no official visitors. She went to bed at eleven o'clock or thereabouts. The dogs were on station. The general was working in his study. At a little past midnight, she was awakened by a disturbance outside. The dogs were snarling and carrying on. There also may have been a gunshot. She's not sure on that point. She ran downstairs and found her uncle slumped in a chair near the fireplace, half of his head blown away. Claims that she fainted, doesn't know how long she was out. Her story comes confused along in here. When she came around again, she says, the dogs were still at it. Suddenly they got quiet. A minute later, this man walks into the study. Are you ready?"

Braddock growled, "I'm ready. Hit me."

"This was a tall man, well built, athletic. She says he walked in like a cat. He was wearing a black combat outfit. Hands and face smeared with some black cosmetic. She further describes him as quote, guns and things strapped all over him, unquote."

Braddock found himself leaning tensely forward in his chair. He said, "Now wait a minute, John."

"No, hear it all first. She—"

"This was *after* she'd found her uncle dead?"

66

"Like I said, it's confused. But's that what she says. The guy walks in, looks at the dead man, gathers up a sheaf of papers from the desk—memoirs, she says—puts them in the fireplace, and sets fire to them. Then he simply walks out."

"Bullshit," Braddock growled.

"That's her story, and we can't shake it."

"Did he leave a marksman's medal at the scene?"

"No."

"Then he didn't kill the man," Braddock declared.

"How can you leap to a conclusion like that?"

"Look, you called me as a Bolan expert, right? I'll leap to any damn conclusion I wish. When Bolan kills he leaves no doubt that he was there."

"Okay, forget that angle for a moment. Maybe Bolan didn't actually kill Winters. Maybe it was a suicide, just as all the evidence indicates. Other than that, Tim . . . does this sound like Bolan?"

"Here and there," Braddock growled. "Did you have the woman look at mugs?"

"Sure. Nothing positive. She said it *could* be the same man. Kept talking about his *eyes*."

Braddock sighed. He said, softly, "Shit."

"Does that mean I've got the problem of the century in my town?"

"First, let me straighten this out. Is the woman saying that the guy was in the house all the while? That he could have been there when Winters died?"

Tatum replied, "No, I didn't get that from her statement. She's apparently convinced that Winters did indeed kill himself. Even said that she had lately been concerned that something like this may happen. Said her uncle had been severely depressed, moody—obviously under some great strain."

"Maybe he knew that Bolan was stalking him," Braddock mused. "Would that be a valid theory?"

"Nothing official," the San Diego cop replied, "but I've heard a few whispers about Winco Industries. They were under investigation once— the federal boys—but apparently nothing came of it."

"You said the dogs were still alive and active when your men got there?"

"Yeah. Very much so. So you tell me, Tim. Is Bolan good enough to climb a hundred feet of sheer rock?"

"He's no fly," Braddock replied thoughtfully. "Did you test the dogs?"

"For what?"

"Drugs."

The line between L.A. and San Diego hummed through a brief silence, then the embarrassed voice from the south admitted, "No. But I'll get a pathologist out there right away."

"That's how he'd do it," Braddock was thoughtfully deciding. "If it were Bolan, he'd know the dogs were there long before he started his move against the place. And he'd come prepared for them. You . . . uh . . . already know, I suppose, about the old connection between Bolan and Winters."

Another embarrassed silence, then: "What connection?"

"We ran a total make on Bolan while he was in our town," Braddock explained. "I talked to Winters myself, part of the routine. He was

68

Bolan's combat C.O. in Vietnam for awhile."

The silence became oppressive. Finally the man in San Diego said, "You never cleared that with me, Tim."

"Sorry, there was no time for niceties. Winters wasn't suspected of any involvement with Bolan at the time. I was just looking for background on the guy. I set up the meet at the Del Mar country club. We had a drink; he told me what he knew about Bolan, supposedly; I thanked him and left. Had a hell of a hot war storming through my own town at the time, you may remember."

"Yeah," came the sour reply. "And now it's an odds-on favorite that I've got one coming up in my town."

"Could be. But don't push the theory too far, John. The impression I got from Winters, I recall, was that he was holding out on me. The height-weight-serial number routine. He gave me very damned little. Later I discovered via other sources that he and Bolan had been very close friends, forget the difference in rank."

The San Diego cop sighed heavily. He said, quietly, "How about giving me the benefit of your mistakes. If you had it to do over again, how would you have handled your Bolan invasion?"

Braddock replied, "Okay, I accept the dig. But I wouldn't change anything. Except maybe I'd move a bit faster than I did against the mob. I suggest you do that. Hit 'em with anything you can think of, but get them behind bars. And keep them there until the guy gets tired of waiting and drifts on out."

"That's a cop-out."

"Call it what you like. Just remember, Bolan

doesn't stay long in one place. Part of his survival M.O. Hit quick and get out. Disappears for awhile, pops up again far away for another quick hit and git."

"You know how long I can keep these boys behind bars, Tim? Just as long as it takes their damned lawyers to hit me with a briefcase full of legal papers."

"Sure, I know that. So you turn them loose and grab them again as they're climbing into their cars. For spitting on the sidewalk, for making an obscene gesture, for sweating. And you keep it up until—"

"Yeah I know the routine," Tatum declared wearily.

"I don't know what else to tell you, John."

"You told me precisely what I did *not* want you to tell me, Tim."

Braddock said, "Maybe the Winters girl is more confused than you think. I'll say this much: it doesn't sound like the usual Bolan thing. I mean, when the guy hits your town, you seldom have to wonder if he's really there."

"So I hear," Tatum commented sourly.

Another voice entered the telephone hookup, a voice which sounded as though it were accustomed to respectful listening. "Captain Braddock. This is Chief Larson."

Braddock said, "Yes sir."

"I'm sitting across the desk from John. Excuse me for not announcing my presence earlier but I thought it better that you approach the question without official intimidation. It's time for that now. You're considered the foremost authority in the West on the Bolan problem. I'm asking you

70

now for an official opinion. Is the Executioner operating in this city?"

Braddock sighed. "I'd have to say, yes sir, it sounds that way. He'll probably confirm it, very loudly, at most any time now."

"All right. I'll be talking to your chief but I suppose I should clear it with you first. I'd like you down here with us, in an advisory capacity."

It was getting to be a habit. Braddock had hardly unpacked from the trek to Boston.

He sighed and told the San Diego official, "I'll have to beg off, Sir. My work here is stacked up around my ears. I think we could spring another man, though—and, actually, he's been much closer to Bolan than I have."

"I don't want you unless you're willing, Captain. You won't reconsider?"

"I'm sorry, sir. The department wouldn't allow it even if I wanted to go. If you'll make the request via official channels, though, I'll see that you're provided the best man available."

"All right. I'll rely on that, Captain."

Tatum chimed in with, "Tim, thanks."

"You bet," Braddock replied, and broke the connection.

He immediately poked his intercom and told his secretary, "Run down Sergeant Lyons for me—Carl Lyons. He should be in Organized Crime Division. Tell him to grab a toothbrush and be in my office within the hour. Then set me up for five minutes in the Chief's office—make it urgent business conference—and request that Captain Mira of OCD be present."

"Sounds like a bell-ringer," the secretary commented.

"You better believe it. Oh—and when you're talking to Sergeant Lyons—tell him it's a *Hardcase*."

"I thought *Hardcase* was dead."

"Not yet," Braddock growled into the intercom. "It's apparently alive and well . . . in San Diego."

Thank God.

Thank God it was not Braddock's problem this time.

7: DANGER'S FOLLY

They were supposed to have gotten underway at seven o'clock and here it was eight already. If they were going to cancel these goddamn things, why the hell didn't somebody have enough thought about them to let a guy know it was off?

Gene (the Turtle) Tarantini paced the glistening deck of the flying bridge and ranted inwardly at the sorry way things had been going lately with this chicken outfit.

He'd rather be back in the navy . . . almost. Not quite. But there wasn't much difference . . . when a guy got to thinking about it. Same damn chicken outfit. Guys pulling rank all the time, giving out orders right and left, expecting you to snap-shit every time they stepped aboard.

Let Tony Danger run his own fuckin' navy!

He stepped over to the voice tube and blew into

it to attract attention down below, then he announced, "Hear this, you fucking muddy-water sailors. The admiral has not been piped aboard and it don't look like he's coming. Secure the fucking engines—hey wait, belay that. I think his imperial lateness has finally arrived."

A guy was coming down the steps from the sun deck of the marina's lounge. White bell bottoms, deck shoes, knit shirt, bright yellow nylon windbreaker and the inevitable skipper's hat. Dark sun glasses. Carrying a briefcase.

The Turtle turned back to the voice tube and passed the word to his two-man crew. "Look alive, you know how his feelings get hurt if we don't show no sideboys."

Then he picked up the binoculars and took a closer look.

Hell, that wasn't Tony Danger.

Too tall, too big all over. Too much of everything.

But the guy was sure headed for *Danger's Folly*, no doubt about that. And he sure looked like the real article. That briefcase was chained to his wrist.

Tarantini put down the binoculars and swung into the cockpit of the big cruiser. He pulled a .38 revolver from the chart case, checked it, spun the cylinder, and replaced it.

"Watch it," he growled down to the two men who were just then emerging from the cabin. "Something's not exactly kosher here."

Bolan had picked up the outfit at the Mission Bay "Mariner's Shop"—and he suspected that

74

Tony Danger had bought his seagoing togs at the same place; there'd been no difficulty whatever in duplicating the outfit, right down to the fancy sunglasses with little anchors at the posts.

He spotted the guy watching him through binoculars from the cruiser and knew that he was being closely scrutinized.

It was a beautiful hunk of seagoing mahogany, definitely in the yacht class. Powerful, sleek. Must have cost a bundle.

By the time he reached the gangway, two more guys in spotless T-shirts and white ducks were standing at the rail in a sort of self-conscious parade-rest stance. Each wore a navy-style white hat, rakishly cocked over the eyes, the sidebands flaring out in the center like wings.

Bolan stepped aboard and gave the sailors an impatient toss of his head. "We're late," he growled. "Cast off, haul that gangway in."

A voice from above him snarled, "I give the fucking orders aboard here, sir."

Bolan angled his gaze toward the flying bridge and told the little guy up there, "You'll be giving orders up your ass if you don't get this tub moving."

The guy grinned at him and, in a much milder tone, asked, "Where's Mr. Danger?"

Bolan did not return the smile. His voice was softer, though, in the reply. "Something's rumbling. There might be trouble. Tony's sitting this one out with th' boss." He shook the briefcase. "Do we go or don't we?"

The man on the bridge raised a bos'n's pipe to his lips and tootled a shrieking command through it.

Bolan grinned on that one and watched the crewmen scramble expertly through the casting-off exercises. A moment later the cruiser was moving smoothly through the smallcraft harbor and heading for open water.

He went up and joined the man at the conn, watched him in silence for a moment, then told him, "I'm Frankie Lambretta. Who're you?"

The guy gave him a dazzling smile and replied, "I'm Gene Tarantini. Mr. Danger started calling me "Turtle"—now everybody does. You may as well, too."

"Okay." Bolan ran his hands along Tarantini's body in a quick frisk, then growled, "Hey, I told you there might be trouble. Where the hell's your hardware?"

The guy glanced toward the chart case and said, "In there."

Bolan commanded, "Wear it!"

"Yessir."

"Do your boys have hardware?"

"Yessir, we keep it down in the quarters."

"I can handle the wheel for a minute," Bolan said. "You go tell those boys to get dressed."

Tarantini flashed another big smile, turned the wheel over to his passenger and descended quickly to the main deck. He was back seconds later, reaching into the chart case and tucking a revolver into the waistband of his trousers. He said, almost shyly, "You're a real torpedo, aren't you."

Bolan relinquished the conn and growled, "Yeh."

"I knew it the minute I saw you. I ain't seen a dude like you since Manhattan. You don't take no orders from Mr. Danger, do you?"

Bolan made a derisive sound.

"I thought not. You're class, Mr. Lambretta . . . real class."

"Thanks," Bolan said. He was silent for a moment, then he told the impressionable *Mafioso*, "Listen, Turtle, I might be sliding into something very uncomfortable. You know?"

"Yessir. I already figured that."

"I'll appreciate some close support from you and your boys, if things get to that."

"Yessir, you can count on that."

"Okay. You've got a sharp crew here. Stay that way."

"You offer odds on that, Mr. Lambretta."

Bolan punched the guy lightly on the shoulder and went below to the main deck.

The Ventura Boulevard bridge was just ahead.

In a few minutes they would be in open sea.

Where to from there?

It was a wild-ass play he was making. He knew that. So . . . why change the name of the game now? His entire life had become a wild-ass play.

He walked toward the stern and reached into his armpit to activate the miniature shoulder phone, then turned his face to the side and shielded his mouth with a hand as he spoke into the sensitive microphone. "Gadgets."

"Yo."

"Anything?"

"Plenty. Are you clear?"

"For the moment. What do you have?"

"Our young lady called a lot of people and said a lot of screwy things. The one you'll be most interested in is a guy she called Max. You tie that?"

Bolan replied, "I tie. Our VIP. That's a fast bingo."

"Yeah. Faster than you'll know until you've screened this stuff. It's too much for a quick report. Where are you?"

"Aboard *Danger's Folly,* heading for open sea."

"God! What's the lie?"

"I decided to make that buy for Tony."

"God! Hope you know what you're doing."

"Me too, Gadgets. Off. Don't beep me. I'll check in soon as I'm back on dry land."

"Do that. I'll be monitoring."

Bolan repeated, "Off," and deactivated the radio. He lit a cigarette and strolled casually toward the bow.

He noticed the two crewmen perched tensely at the rail on the starboard side, each displaying the butt of a revolver in the waistband of their bell-bottoms, watching him as though he were a prize exhibit at some zoo.

He went on to the bow and leaned out to watch the water swirling past.

Yeah.

He hoped he knew what he was doing.

In all truth, though, he had not the faintest idea of where he was going or what he would do when he got there.

Danger's Folly, hell!

It was very possibly going to prove *Bolan's* folly . . . and that was the brutal truth of that.

8: THE BUY

They'd been underway for nearly an hour and—
to Bolan's best calculation—on a due-west heading. There'd been no conversation between Bolan
and the crew. He had not encouraged any, but
spent the early time prowling the boat to get the
feel of it.

The main cabin—marked "Salon" with a brass
plaque above the doorway—was done up for solid
creature comforts. It was not overly large, but a
lot of entertaining could be done in there. Couches
and chairs, he noted, converted to sleeping ar-
rangements for eight.

The engine room was crammed full of the most
impressive-looking power plant Bolan had ever
seen. It was quietly and smoothly propelling the
big boat through the heavy swells of the open sea
at a very respectable cruising speed.

The crews' quarters were housed in a small cabin behind the engine room. Four bunks, adequate headroom, small galley and lounge area—all of it clean and neatly shipshape.

The familiarization completed, Bolan sprawled into a deck chair on the fantail and watched the churning wake billow out beneath him.

They must have been twenty-five miles or so out when Bolan spotted the other boat. It was a classy speedster, deep draft, done up for sports fishing and flying a line of pennants from the mast.

He left his chair immediately and headed casually toward the bridge. Tarantini was inspecting the other boat through binoculars. He lowered the glasses as Bolan walked up and handed them to him.

"That's her," Tarantini announced. "And ready to deal."

They were still about a mile away.

Bolan growled, "How do you know?"

"Those pennants. It's a signal meaning everything's okay. If the Coast Guard or anything else suspicious had been in the area recently, she'd be flying a warning signal."

Bolan nodded. He said, "Okay, let's go."

They were running on the other boat's beam, passing to the rear now.

"We're going," Tarantini assured his passenger. "We don't just run right up to them, y'know. But you can relax. I don't see no signs of trouble."

"You won't until we get there," Bolan warned. "Tell your boys to stay alert. And you run with my play. Understand?"

The Turtle smiled soberly. "You expecting some kind of double-cross?"

"Maybe something like that," the Executioner replied, and turned his full attention to a binocular surveillance of his target.

Five minutes later *Danger's Folly* was coming alongside the other boat, sliding in from the starboard quarter. She was marked *Pepe* and, beneath the name, *Ensenada*.

A Mexican registry.

Undoubtedly the rendezvous was taking place in international waters.

Bolan had to give Tarantini due credit. He knew his boat handling. It was a delicate maneuver; boats in open sea did not handle like rolling objects on a stable surface. They slid, wallowed, lunged and leaped. Both boats were maintaining sufficient headway for maneuverability, moving along at a speed of about ten knots. Horizontal separation was only about twenty feet, but both were maintaining station beautifully.

Bolan counted four Mexican crewmen, including the guy at the wheel. Standing beside the Mexican skipper was a beefy, red-faced man wearing slacks and a gaudy sports shirt, no hat, partially bald. American . . . or European.

The sailors were throwing lines across and setting up a transfer operation, the usual nautical bit of pulleys and control lines.

Tarantini's full attention was being absorbed by the demanding job at the wheel. Without looking at Bolan, he told him, "Okay, we're on station. You can do your thing now."

Bolan had already noticed that his counterpart aboard the *Pepe* was moving toward the main deck. He took his cue from that and descended the ladder, dropping beside the two crewmen near the transfer lines. One of them silently handed him a battery-powered megaphone.

Bolan growled, "Watch those bastards."

The crewman nodded understandingly and stepped aside.

The guy on the *Pepe's* dealing deck had a bull-horn also. He called across, in a strong French accent, "Where is *M'sieur* Danger?"

"Couldn't make it," Bolan horned back. "You got the stuff?"

"My arrangement was with *M'sieur* Danger."

"Then go deal with him," Bolan replied. He raised the attache case. "But what counts is right here."

"You have one hundred American?"

"That was the deal, wasn't it," Bolan called back.

"And five for the *Pepe*."

"Yeah, sure. I gotta check the stuff first, though."

The Frenchman dug into a rubberized bag and produced a small packet which he passed to a seaman beside him. The sample went into a trans-fer basket and moved smoothly across the twenty intervening feet of Pacific.

Bolan removed it from the basket and opened the small plastic bag. He touched his tongue to the white powder in there. It was pure heroin, or damned close to pure. A hundred-thousand worth of the stuff would produce a million-buck's worth of street junk.

He raised the bullhorn and demanded, "Let's see the rest of it."

"I would see the color of your American first."

Bolan obligingly opened the attache case and pulled out a packet of bills. He dropped them in the basket and gave the signal to the sailors. As it was making the transit, he called over, "That's the five for the *Pepe*. The rest is just like it."

The guy was already inspecting the money.

He was smiling as he announced, "Okay. We have the deal. Send over the hundred."

"You send over the stuff first."

The smile evaporated as the Frenchman, visibly upset, called back, "This is not the way. *M'sieur* Tony Danger has never done business this way. You pay, I deliver. This is the way."

Bolan replied, "So I'll pay."

He reached into the attache case again, but this time his fist came out filled with a big silver pistol, the .44 AutoMag, and it spoke instantly in a big rolling boom as the magnum missile dissolved the distance between the Executioner and his target.

The Frenchman received his payment at the rail and his head exploded in receipt.

The Mexican seamen stood in stunned stupor and watched the lifeless body spin over the rail and into the water between the boats.

The AutoMag was at full extension and staring down on them when Bolan's taut voice again crackled through the bullhorn: "You *amigos* have your five thousand American and that's all you were in it for! Do the smart thing and send that junk on over here!"

The skipper of the *Pepe*, like the American skipper, had his hands full with the delicate job of maintaining station. He had undoubtedly seen little of what had transpired between the two boats, but obviously he had heard enough. A shouted command in Spanish came down from the bridge and the stunned sailors reacted instantly, stuffing the Frenchman's rubberized bag into the transfer basket and hauling away on the line.

A *Folly* sailor snatched the precious cargo from the basket.

Bolan yelled, "Cast off and haul ass!"

Turtle was already into the play, however. The *Folly* swung suddenly to starboard and the lines parted with a twanging snap as they veered away from the other boat's course.

A moment later, two unbelieving American sailors watched "Frankie Lambretta" slash packet after packet of high grade heroin and scatter the precious powders into the blue Pacific.

"Trash," he told them, when the job was completed. "The guy was trying to sell us trash."

And one hour later, when he was making his goodbyes to the admiring crew of *Danger's Folly*, he told Turtle Tarantini: "You run a tight ship, Skipper. I'll mention it to the boss."

With a look approaching open adoration, the *Mafioso* told the Executioner, "Mr. Lambretta, you're the classiest guy I've ever had the pleasure to meet."

Yeah.

So okay.

It hadn't turned into *Bolan's* Folly, after all.

And the world would hardly miss an international junk salesman and a million bucks worth of human misery.

The *mob* would, sure.

And that, of course, was the name of the immediate game: *Siege*. He would lock them out and shut them out at every turn.

And then, maybe, something interesting would come up over the hill. A target, maybe, in the *Big Middle*.

9: DISCOVERY

"Where the hell you been with my boat?" Tony Danger screamed from the pier as *Danger's Folly* came alongside.

Tarantini ignored the emotional greeting while he completed the docking procedure, and not until she was tied-up and the engines secured did he move to the wing of the bridge to grin down at his boss on the pier.

"Come on aboard, sir," he called down. "Mr. Lambretta left you a report."

Anthony Cupaletto, or "Tony Danger" as he had become known in mob circles, was not a man given to vague fears or unreasonable worries. He had started in the business fifteen years earlier as a paid-gun guarding the person of Julian DiGeorge, then boss of the Southern California underworld. His cool efficiency and loyalty to the great man

86

had not gone unnoticed or unrewarded, and Tony Danger had moved quickly along the happy road to wealth and prestige in the DiGeorge organization. The thirty-five-year-old was now regarded in ranking circles as the ambitious young man to watch out for in the ever-shifting power structures of the times.

Cool, shrewd, hard, dependable—Tony Danger seemed destined to go a long way in the business.

So, no, he was not normally a fearful **or** an anxious man.

At this particular moment, however, he was both.

He ignored the gangway which the crewmen were emplacing, leapt onto the deck of his pride and joy, then went quickly up to join his skipper on the bridge.

"Mister *who* left me *what?*" he growled at Tarantini.

"Mr. Lambretta," the Turtle repeated. The look on the boss's face was destroying his self-confidence and his voice was showing the stress. "You know . . . Frankie Lambretta, Mr. Lucasi's hard arm. Hell, you should've *seen* that guy operate."

The name meant something to Tony Danger . . . *Lambretta* . . . wasn't that . . . ?

It hit him then and—his worst fears suddenly surfacing in the pit of his gut—Danger covered his consternation by shoving a cigarette between his lips and leaning into the lee of the flying bridge to light it.

Sure. That was what he'd called himself at Palm Springs.

Frankie Lucky.

Frankie Lucky Lambretta.

Mack fuckin' Bolan!

The San Diego *caporegime* exhaled a gusty cloud of smoke and quietly asked his skipper, "What the hell are you telling me, Turtle?"

"You didn't know about it?" Tarantini asked nervously.

"About *what?*" Tony Danger growled, working hard to control his emotions.

"He said he was supposed to make the buy at the *Pepe*. He said there was trouble, and *he* was going instead of *you*. He said—"

"*Fuck* what he *said!*" Tony Danger yelled. "What did he *do?*"

Tarantini took a retreating half-step in the face of that rage and choked out: "Hell I thought you knew. I thought it was cleared through you. The Frenchman tried to pass some bad stuff. Mr. Lambretta drilled him and dumped the junk."

"He did *what?*" Tony Danger screamed.

Turtle Tarantini looked about ready to run. Instead he thrust forward a heavy manila envelope, pushing it towards his boss. "I guess it's all in here," he said weakly. "He said give this to you."

Tony Danger accepted the "report" but his eyes remained hot and unbelieving on his skipper. "Where is this guy right now?" he wanted to know.

"He had us drop him on the other side. Said his car was over there."

"When?"

"Five, maybe ten minutes ago."

Tony Danger did not wish to open that envelope. He knew, he thought, what was in there.

He muttered, "He dumped the stuff?"

"Yessir. It was trash. He paid the *Pepe* for their run, but he put a bullet right between the Frenchman's eyes. Mr. Danger, that guy knew what he was doing. Believe me."

"Fifty kilos," Tony Danger muttered. "A million bucks on the streets. He *dumped* it?"

"I told you, it was *trash*. I thought you knew all about that. I thought...."

"You think too much, Turtle," Tony Danger told his uncomfortable skipper. He was opening the envelope—slowly, delicately.. "You're gonna fool around and think yourself into an early grave. You *think* about *that*."

Turtle Tarantini's eyes clearly did not understand his boss's reaction to the superb job Frankie Lambretta had done for him.

"Too many people give orders around here," he muttered defensively.

Tony Danger did not hear the remark.

He was staring into the brown manila envelope.

He dug a finger into a small sample of white powder in there and touched it to his tongue.

"Trash, eh?" he commented miserably.

Then he withdrew the little iron cross with a bull's-eye in its center and showed it to his skipper.

"That's your Frankie Lambretta," he said in a flat voice.

"I don't believe it," Tarantini whispered.

"You'd better," Tony Danger quietly told him. "You'd damn sure better believe it."

He turned away to conceal the quivering of his lips and quickly descended the ladder to the main deck.

Damn right.

Everybody had better start believing it.
Hell had finally come to San Diego.

Bolan established radio contact with Gadgets
Schwarz to set up a rendezvous where he could
screen the intelligence from the telephone tap on
the Winters residence, but Blancanales broke into
the conversation with an urgent report of his own.

"Been hoping you'd check in pretty quick," the
Politician told his C.O. "All hell is breaking around
here. My subject has had people coming and going
ever since I reached station. It smells of a build-up
and I want you to look at some pictures I took
with the Polaroid."

Bolan had a vast respect for the judgement of
the combat-intelligence expert. His decision was
quick and positive. "Change the game plan," he
replied. "Remain on station and cover Gadgets
for his intel run. Gadgets, start your drain operation in exactly ten minutes. Pol, follow him out.
I'll be covering from Station Charlie. Regroup
with all caution at Point Alpha."

It was beginning to size up as a rather short
siege.

The enemy, it seemed, was already gearing for
the break-out.

The emergency conference had been shaping up
for better than an hour. The key men from Mexico
had arrived and the boys from the California
desert interior were expected at any moment.
Additionally, a four-point telephone conference

was being set up on scrambler circuits with New York, Phoenix, and Los Angeles.

Ben Lucasi was not letting any Bolan dust settle on *him*. Maybe the other bosses around the country were reluctant to yell for help when the bastard came crashing in on them—not Big Ben Lucasi. He had been accorded the "Big" tag not by virtue of his physical dimensions but by the size of his ambitions and ideas.

And Big Ben Lucasi did not take *this* brand of crap from anybody.

When the telephone sounded off, he'd thought it to be the scrambler conference coming through ... but it was only Tony Danger.

"What th' hell, hang up," Lucasi ordered. "I'm expecting the national wire."

"Here's something maybe you weren't expecting," his lieutenant advised him. "That goddam Bolan came out here and conned my boat crew into taking him out to sea. He hit our French connection, bumped the guy, scattered the shipment on the high seas. Whattaya think of that, Ben? A million fuckin' bucks giving the fishes a thrill."

"Th' rotten bastard!" Lucasi muttered angrily. "What the hell d'you think he's pulling this crap for?"

"Well, he's not just tweaking our noses," Tony Danger assured the boss. "Bet your ass, he's got something very serious on his mind."

"Awright, you get it on over here!" Lucasi demanded. "We're about ready to go to council. Listen, Tony, we're going to put an end to this bullshit here and now. You say he killed Beloit?"

"Yeah. And there went four hard months of

sweat and tears. I tell you, Ben, this stuff is getting hard to come by. We just can't afford to lose good brokers this way."

"I know, I know," Lucasi replied, commiserating with his favorite lieutenant. "Well look, get it on back here. We'll take care of Mr. Smart-ass for good and all."

"Be there in ten minutes," Tony Danger promised, and hung up.

The delegates to the convention were all in the game room, quietly consoling their ruffled nerves with the best booze from the Lucasi liquor closet. He hold his house captain, the Diver, "I'll be in there with the boys. That call comes through, you send it right in on the squawk box."

"I just come in to tell you," Diver said, "that something funny is going on outside."

"What d'you mean, funny?"

"If you got just a second, I'd like to show you."

Lucasi followed his chief bodyguard to the patio, his guts shivering just a little under this new "funny" business.

The big guy was pointing up the street. "See that bread truck up there . . . up inna next block?"

Lucasi growled, "Yeah. So what?"

"So it's been in this neighborhood for the past two hours."

"Is the guy making deliveries?"

"Seems to be. But, hell, how long can a guy spend in one neighborhood?"

"Depends," Lucasi replied, with a stab at humor, "on how many stud-hungry housewives he's servicing, I guess. Is that what you brought me out here for?"

"That's not all." The Diver swiveled about to

92

sight along his outstretched arm in the opposite direction. "See that up there?"

"I see a little green truck," the boss replied, with some irritation. "So what?"

"So I seen the same damn truck over on the next street earlier this morning. Right after we got hit."

Lucasi was attempting to appear unruffled. He drawled, "All right, I never accused you of bad instincts, Diver. What d'you think is so funny about this?"

"I think maybe we're being watched."

"Oh?" Lucasi thrust a cigar between his teeth and chewed on it for a few seconds, then said, "There was sure something funny about that hit here this morning. You thinking that, too?"

The Diver soberly nodded his head. "It just isn't like Bolan."

"He hit the *Pepe* awhile ago," Lucasi confided, *sotto voce*. "Bumped Beloit and dumped our shipment in the ocean."

"Sounds like he's getting smarts somewheres," Diver muttered. His eyes were roaming the exterior of the house. "He could've bumped *you*, Mr. Lucasi, as easy as anything. I keep wondering why he didn't."

"I guess maybe he just wasn't ready to," Lucasi replied in a strained voice. The tension was wearing through again. He loudly cleared his throat and added, "I guess he had something else on his mind." Lucasi was following the scan of his house captain's gaze. The hairs rose along the back of his neck. "Are you thinking what I'm thinking?" he growled.

"Well, we know he's not working alone this

93

time," Diver quietly replied. His arm rose and he pointed toward a second-floor window. "Do you see something up there? On that ledge there, by the window?"

Lucasi's blood almost stopped flowing. "Shake this fuckin' place down," he commanded, almost choking with the effort at speech. "I mean *good* and *fast!*"

The house captain took off on a run, loudly calling his boys together as he went.

Lucasi hurried after him, tremblingly intent upon clearing that open area with all speed.

"Suckered!" he muttered to himself. "Sonuvabitch!"

For damn sure. The bastard had suckered him with the oldest trick in the books.

But maybe it wasn't too late to pull the fat out of the fire. Maybe, by God, Mr. Smart-ass would find his own fat searing in the flames this time.

"Those trucks!" he screamed. "Get out there and grab them trucks!"

10: POINT BLANK

Bolan was watching from a high point of ground which was several blocks removed from the Lucasi home, following the play there with powerful binoculars.

He had been on station and waiting when Schwarz began his intelligence run in the warwagon, had watched him pull up to within fifty yards of the target and dismount, open the hood over the engine, step inside the van.

He saw Blancanales, also, another hundred yards or so downrange, inching along in the bread truck.

Bolan spoke into his shoulder-phone to advise, "Pol, the ears are out."

"Roger, I have him in sight," came the instant reply. "How's it look from station Charlie?"

"Peaceful," Bolan said, then: "Whup! Couple

just came out the side door. It's . . . Lucasi. And the big houseman. Something has their interest."

The focal field of the binoculars covered only the two men and several feet of turf to either side of them.

"I believe they're looking at *you*, Pol. And . . . Gadgets! Are you in?"

"I'm here," came a strained reply.

"They've spotted both of you, and I'd say are jumping to conclusions. I can feel their little minds a'whirring. Yep. Yep."

Lucasi's weasel face was sharply etched in the focal field, wondering, worrying, *discovering* . . .

Bolan commanded, "Break off! They're wise. Break *now!*"

Schwarz protested, "I only drained two banks."

"Got the phone tap?"

"Getting it now."

"Stay with it," Blancanales urged. "I'm covering."

Bolan concurred, though with misgivings. Numbers were all-important in this sort of game. He snapped, "Thirty seconds more, then you haul it! Pol, start your move!"

"Rolling," came the response from Blancanales.

Bolan released the binoculars and reached for his power sniper, the Weatherby Mark V. Using .460 Magnum soft-nose mini-bombs, the big piece gave him better than a thousand yards of kill— much more than he would need for this mission. He fitted his eye to the scope and began reading ranges.

Yeah . . . this mission would be just about point-blank.

Micronite filter.
Mild, smooth taste.
For all the right reasons.
Kent.

America's quality cigarette.
King Size or Deluxe 100's.

Micronite filter.
Mild, smooth taste.
For all the right reasons.
Kent.

Regular or Menthol.

Kings: 17 mg. "tar,"
1.1 mg. nicotine;
100's: 19 mg. "tar,"
1.3 mg. nicotine;
Menthol: 19 mg. "tar,"
1.3 mg. nicotine
av. per cigarette,
FTC Report Aug. '72.

The Diver sent three of his boys out to intercept the bread truck and another two to check-out the green van, then he sent the remaining palace guard scurrying through the house searching for bugs.

Ben Lucasi ran into the game room to caution everyone there to "keep quiet, stop talking, not a fucking word!"—then he snatched up a double-barrel shotgun and dashed toward the upstairs window where he'd spotted the suspicious-looking package.

He arrived there just in time to see the bread truck picking up speed for a run past the house.

Three of Diver's boys were chasing along beside it, waving pistols and shouting at one another.

A burst of fire from an automatic weapon lanced away from the cab of the truck and the three boys went down sliding in their own blood.

The truck had slowed again, almost coming to a complete halt near the front of the property, and the automatic-weapon fire was sweeping into the house itself as that damned guy down there methodically raked the whole joint. Window glass was breaking and crashing all over; Lucasi could hear yelling and stampeding feet as his visitors sought cover. Above it all, the loud commands of big Diver could be heard as the veteran house captain tried to get his forces deployed against the unexpected assault.

Without even realizing what a foolish thing he was doing, Lucasi shattered his window with the shotgun, leaned out, and let go with both barrels into that bread truck.

The double *ba-loom* of his own retort was echoed instantly far away by the powerful reports from a big-game piece. Something tore the shotgun out of Lucasi's grasp and sent it spinning to the ground; something else smacked into the window frame a fraction of an inch from his eyes and tore a foot of it away.

Lucasi fell back quickly into the safety of the room, his hands still tingling from the hit on his shotgun, and he knew that he'd come as close to sudden death as he ever wanted to get.

He scrambled down the stairway yelling, "Diver! Diver!"

But the Diver was already outside, leading his pack of triggermen in a hard run across the yard, taking the battle exactly where Mack Bolan probably wanted it.

"Don't go out there!" Lucasi wailed.

Too late.

Another rattling sound from up the street signalled the entrance of a second automatic weapon into the battle, and the rolling *cra-acks* of that big-game piece were now coming end-to-end, almost sounding as one.

Yeah, Lucasi knew it. It was too damn late now.

Bolan had been watching for a response to Blancanales' stutter-pistol attack, and he saw the shotgun the moment it presented itself outside that upstairs window.

He immediately acquired that target in his cross-hairs and sighed into the squeeze-off, realizing as he did so that he was at least a heartbeat behind the other guy's trigger. His own piece bucked into his shoulder at the same instant that the report from the shotgun reached him; he rode

98

the recoil and hung into the eyepiece for another quick round into the same general target area.

The intense magnification of the big scope provided a field of vision measuring in inches but he saw the shotgun take the hit and spin away, and he had a milli-second glimpse of Ben Lucasi's frightened visage jerking away from a splintering windowframe.

He paused then for an area-evaluation with the binoculars.

Blancanales had abandoned the bread truck. Apparently the shotgun blast had disabled the vehicle.

Two men were in the street, about midway between the house and Schwarz's position with the warwagon. At the moment they seemed to be torn between their original assignment and the obvious need for their presence back at the house.

Bolan barked into the shoulder-phone, "Pol, Gadgets, report!"

Blancanales came in immediately, a bit winded, "I'm grounded, two o'clock from the front of the house, behind the little rock wall."

"I'm done," Gadgets announced calmly. "Get ready, Pol, I'll pick you up."

"Negative!" Bolan commanded. "You do a one-eighty and haul out of there. I'll spring the Politician."

"Too late," Schwarz replied. "Here come the reserves."

Bolan snarled, "It still goes. You break and haul —backwards!"

"Aye aye."

"I'm okay," Blancanales assured everybody.

99

With his naked eye Bolan could see that the Politician would not be "okay" for long.

A swarm of hardmen were pouring out of the house and making a cautious advance toward the street.

As he was leaning into his eyepiece, he heard the stutter of Schwarz's weapon and got a peripheral glimpse of the two men in the street as they dived for cover. One of them did not dive quite soon enough; Bolan saw him flop and roll, then he sighed into his own targets. Gadgets, he knew, could take care of himself.

As for those guys down there in that yard . . . at this range, with this piece, it was almost a shame. Even scrambling, they were sitting ducks.

He was in a tight spot, and the Politician damn well knew it.

The little NATO machine pistol had jammed on him and there was no time to work on it. He had a damn revolver and six lousy rounds between him and about fifteen guys who were moving across that lawn over there.

His closest help was damn near one hundred yards away, and *he* had been ordered out of the area.

The Sarge, of course, was laying-in with the big precision piece—and that fact would not prove at all comforting to anyone moving into those crosshairs.

Blancanales had confidence in Bolan. If the guy said he'd spring him, then he'd spring him. Still . . . this was not the most enviable of all possible circumstances for a life-loving dude like Rosario Blancanales. And he had not seen the Sarge at work for quite awhile. A guy, even a Mack Bolan, could sometimes lose his numbers.

He watched a group of hardmen splinter off from the main force and start a movement toward Schwarz in the warwagon just as Gadgets opened fire on the two guys already up there. Then the big booms from Bolan's Weatherby began rocking the air again.

The guy could sure tickle a trigger.

Hell, he was firing from about three blocks away but those people over there were going down like clockwork. Blancanales watched them depart the field of combat forever—one, two, three, four —like a cadence count—and those who were left were already beginning to get a whole new slant on the art of warfare.

Some guy was standing in a doorway over there and screaming at them to get back inside.

Bolan's cool voice came through his shoulder-phone then: "Make your move, Pol. Fall back to the next street behind you and hold there. Gadgets, circle around and pick him up."

"Aye, aye," said Gadgets.

"Wilco," Blancanales responded, sighing.

Hell. He'd known all along that the Sarge would spring him. He hadn't lost any damn numbers.

The big question now, of course, was could the *Sarge* spring *himself*.

The wail of police sirens was beginning to crowd the area, boring in from several directions.

Two more big booms erupted from that distant firing-drop and Blancanales, glancing over his shoulder, saw the bread truck explode into flames.

He grinned, aware that Bolan was simply adding a confusion-factor to the scene.

Sure. The guy would spring himself.

11: WAR ZONE

Captain Tatum threaded his way through the congregation of official vehicles and came to a halt at the edge of the war zone.

There was no better way to describe the scene there.

The shattered and burning vehicle in the middle of the street.

Bullet-riddled house, shattered glass, abandoned weapons lying about.

A team of medics moving grimly among the dead and the dying.

Firefighters and uniformed policemen everywhere the eye could see.

The uniformed watch officer spotted the Captain, then came over to offer a report. Tatum recognized him as George Gonzales, a twenty-year veteran with the department—a good man.

"Hell walked through here," Gonzales told the homicide chief. "Seven dead, four stretcher cases, two walking wounded. House is pretty well shot up." He glanced toward the gutted bread truck. "Lot of toast in there, but nothing else. We haven't found the driver. So far all of the victims have been identified as Lucasi's people. Somebody really hit 'im hard, Captain."

"What does the little big man have to say about all this?" Tatum asked musingly.

"He's reserving comment until his attorney arrives. Also refuses to step outside the house— or to show himself at any window . . . with a hundred cops walking around here. . . ."

"He get hurt?"

"No sir, just his dignity. I'd say he's working his way toward a stroke or something, though."

Tatum quickly squelched a wry smile and instructed the watch officer, "Let me know as soon as the lawyer gets here."

"Yes sir. We'll be making charges?"

"You find anything yet to make a book?" the Captain inquired.

"No sir, frankly nothing. It was a one-sided battle, by all appearances. All the firing seems to have come from the other side, whoever they were. Rival gang, looks like. But I haven't even found a weapons violation on Lucasi. All his people are duly licensed as security personnel."

That last was obviously a sore point with Tatum. He screwed his face into a scowl and said, "Yeah, that's nice and neat. How about witnesses?"

"We're working the neighborhood now. So far only one has voluntarily come forward. Lady directly across the street, a Mrs. Bergman. Saw part of it from a bathroom window. Said a man in a white uniform of some kind was crouched behind her wall—" Gonzales paused to point out the spot. "—directly across, there. Said he ran through her property toward the rear just about the time the shooting stopped."

Tatum was scowling toward the burned-out truck, obviously trying to draw conclusions. A small two-way radio at his waist beeped and he reluctantly took time out to answer the call.

"Air Ten has picked up the L.A. special advisor at Lindberg and now has him aboard," was the report. "Do you want him up there?"

"Yeah," Tatum growled. "Give the pilot the general area and tell him to just look for the battleground. He can't miss it."

Gonzales was staring at the Captain as though he wished to know more about this development. Tatum was not yet ready to turn the thing into a circus, however. He knew how the press loved to latch onto a Bolan hit, and he was not quite prepared to go that route. He smiled thinly at the watch officer and told him, "Could be some connection between this and a case up in L.A. awhile back. We're getting a consultant."

This explanation seemed to satisfy the uniformed officer.

The police helicopter was already in sight, wheeling up from the southwest. Tatum watched the little bird come in and settle onto the front lawn, then he went forward to greet the tall young man who had been dispatched from Los Angeles.

The self-introductions were perfunctory and curt, being shouted above the din of the helicopter

—but Tatum was sizing up Sgt. Carl Lyons of L.A.'s Organized Crime Division, and he liked what he saw . . . intelligent, quick, a lawman with a personal commitment.

As soon as the helicopter and its noise had departed the area, Tatum told the new arrival, "I'm only a minute or two ahead of you so we're starting off even." He introduced Gonzales, who brought Lyons up to date on the preliminary report, then the three of them took a walking tour of the battleground.

They halted beside a sheet-draped lump on the front lawn and the Captain knelt for an inspection of the victim. He pulled the sheet away, studied the corpse for a moment, then went on to the next. After the fourth stop, he commented, "Right through the head, all four of them."

"Massive wounds," Lyons added.

"You said seven dead," Tatum told the watch officer. "Where're the other three?"

Gonzales pointed toward the street. "By the truck."

"Head wounds like these?"

"No sir. Multiple body hits from a small calibre weapon. Looks like they got zipped with a light chopper." He swiveled about to point up the street. "Found two more in the next block, lying along the curb in the street. Not dead yet, but damn near. Same type of wounds, they were zipped."

"You said *six* wounded," Tatum reminded him.

"Yes sir, the others were hit inside the house. They just got unlucky. Wrong place at the right time."

Lyons had moved off to the side and was doing a 360-degree survey of the surrounding terrain.

106

His attention became riveted to a pair of distant hillocks.

Tatum and Gonzales ambled over to join Lyons, and the watch officer advised, "Forgot to mention, I sent a car up on Sunset Circle to check out a firing report."

Tatum drawled, "Yeah. . . ." He was sighting toward the high ground which was occupying Lyons' attention. "That would be the western knoll," he informed the out-of-towner. "A guy with a telescopic sight and a good rifle could command this whole neighborhood from up there."

"And looking right along the street," Lyons murmured.

"Is Bolan really that good?" Tatum asked him.

"He's that good," the L.A. cop replied.

The watch officer's eyes had flared at the mention of Bolan's name. In a subdued tone he commented, "It'd take a lot of self-confidence to go for the head from that distance. Did I hear you right? Are you saying this is the Executioner's work?"

"That's what we're trying to determine, George," the Captain replied. "Don't talk it around, though. Sergeant Lyons has tangled with the guy before. Hopefully he can give us a jump on identifying the problem." He grinned without humor. "And I guess the Sergeant has good reason to want to nail Bolan, himself."

"Wrong," Lyons murmured.

"What's that?"

"I owe the guy my life. I'm not that anxious to nail him."

Tatum stared at the young cop for a moment before he quietly inquired, "What did they send me? One for my side or one for his?"

"I'll do my job, Cap'n," Lyons assured him. "But I won't lie to you. My heart won't be in it. I told the same thing to Captain Braddock. So if you want me to turn around and go home then I—"

"Do you smell Bolan around here?" Tatum asked brusquely, shutting out firmly that other line of conversation.

"Faintly, but yessir, I do. I'd like to see some more of the evidence and—"

Another detective had come bustling up and the L.A. advisor gave ground to the obviously urgent nature of the intrusion. The newcomer gave Lyons a curious glance then reported to Captain Tatum, "That house is bugged from top to bottom. Real cute stuff. Radio relays, God's sake, planted outside the windows."

Tatum whistled softly under his breath.

Lyons' facial expression did not alter, but his voice had a crackle of interest as he inquired, "Has your department had this place under electronic surveillance?"

Tatum shook his head. "Never could get it cleared. The local feds have been complaining about the same problem. So unless they just went ahead anyway...."

The L.A. cop said, "Could you check that out? I mean, unofficial but damn quick?"

Tatum gave an eye signal to the other detective. The man nodded and hurried back toward the house, then Tatum asked Lyons, "Are you saying that Bolan...?"

Lyons answered the uncompleted question with, "You better believe it."

"I didn't know the guy was that sophisticated," the homicide chief growled.

"He can be as sophisticated as he wants to get. You asked me about Bolan's smell. I can tell you now, it's getting stronger by the minute. I couldn't. . . ."

"You couldn't what," Tatum asked, glancing at Gonzales with a worried frown.

"Well I just couldn't read this hit into Bolan's M.O. First off, he's worked alone ever since the L.A. hit. Secondly, I couldn't see the guy setting up a hit like this. Too risky, too many possible innocent bystanders on the sidelines. But an *intelligence* probe, now . . . yeah, it reads Bolan all the way. He sends someone in close to work the eavesdropping gear—and I'll bet I know the guy he sent, incidentally—while covering him with precision fire capability from way the hell up there in a non-residential area. It would be—"

Tatum interrupted irritably with: "You're saying the guy didn't come out here looking for blood?"

"That's what I'm saying," Lyons replied, coolly meeting the hot gaze being directed at him. "He's just probing now, looking for targets. Once he gets set and locked onto the people he really wants, then your war will suddenly get very hot."

"What the hell do you call *this?*" Tatum flared, spreading his arms in a dramatic compass of the battle zone.

"It's a probe, Cap'n," Lyons replied evenly. "Just a light probe."

"*Jesus Christ!*" the Captain yelled, and stomped off toward the house.

Gonzales turned a grin to the young cop from

L.A. "I think you said the wrong thing," he told him. "I don't know what it is in your town but, in San Diego, seven dead and six wounded is Friday Night Gangbusters. The Captain gets uptight over just *one* homicide."

"He'd better get loose," Lyons muttered. "He hasn't seen anything yet."

12: TRACKS AROUND
THE TAR PIT

Bolan had learned early in his wars that there was no such thing as a casual connection between the mob and the so-called "straight" community. Whether that connection be social, business, political, or simply a chance pairing of golf or tennis partners—Bolan knew enough of Mafia methods to look penetratingly at any contact between the two levels of American society.

There were no off-duty hours for the mob. Its members' were always in there pitching, in business and in pleasure, and they lost no opportunity to extend their area of influence in whatever direction opened to them.

The Mafia was a cancer. It grew and acquired dominance in the same manner as any cancerous growth—by extension—by moving into weakened adjacent matter and absorbing the resources there into its own spreading designs.

A wise man did not provide hospitable accommodations for a cancerous growth within his own body.

But many supposedly wise businessmen had played around with accommodations for the Mafia cancer. Almost without exception, these men were eaten quickly and easily and were either passed on through as excrement or absorbed into the growing body of the cannibal.

The same thing happened to bored socialites who seemed to think that a hoodlum in the drawing room or even in the bedroom, was "chic"—or at least an interesting conversation-piece.

There were also those straight citizens who unwittingly found themselves in a social or business contact with one of "the boys" and then found it too painful or too dangerous to withdraw from that association. Violent intimidation and blackmail were favorite tools of the cannibals; they never hesitated to apply them unsparingly. The end result for these victims was about the same as for all the others—they were used and abused until every resource had been plundered, then absorbed or eliminated.

Much has been said and written to romanticize the American mobster. Bolan had heard the stories concerning their high moral values, their gallantry to women, their concern for the underdog, their patriotism and love of country, their support of charities, their exalted sense of brotherhood and personal ethics within their own organizations, their high ideals regarding family and community.

And it was all sheer hogwash.

Bolan knew them for what they were.

They were rapists, thieves, sadists, terrorists, murderers. The American mobster was a bloated and self-seeking cannibal who answered to no morality which did not serve to feed his savage lusts and voracious appetites.

None of this had anything to do with being Italian. Often it was their Italian relatives and neighbors who suffered the most at the hands of these unconscionable despots.

Bolan was no psychologist or sociologist. He was not even interested in determining the environmental factors which produced priests, artists and mobsters from the same neighborhood or even from the same family.

He would leave those complicated considerations to those who were trained to study such phenomena.

Mack Bolan's mission was to identify the gangsters, to isolate them and to eliminate them. He was not hampered by intellectual moralizing or agonizing over the questions of force and violence, right and wrong, the constitutional rights of wrongdoers or the legal trickery of the American justice system—all of which had been manipulated by the mob into a protective bubble which insulated them from any effective counterattack by the law-enforcement community.

They owned policemen, in high positions and low. They had their own judges, prosecutors, councilmen, assemblymen, congressmen, bureaucrats—the mob had their own "second invisible government" which saw to their protection at every level of American life.

Except for one.

They had no immunity from the Executioner.

Mack Bolan was no zealot—nor was he a romantic idealist. He was a military realist. He had pledged to defend his country against all enemies, external and internal.

The mob was an internal enemy.

He could draw no realistic line of distinction between this enemy and that one.

The Mafia stood as the most visible and dangerous enemy in his area of perception. He would, until he drowned in his own blood or theirs, fight that enemy with every resource at his command.

The threat at San Diego was shaping into one of those confrontations which Bolan had hoped to avoid.

The problem was similar to the routine dilemma of the war in Vietnam: in order to get at the enemy, you often had to destroy an entire friendly town.

Bolan had managed to keep the major thrust of his homefront wars directed into the hardcore operations of the enemy—into their clout routes, the overtly criminal activities, into pitched battles with their armed forces and execution missions against their leaders.

At San Diego, it was beginning to look like the civilian community might be unavoidably involved in the resolution of the problem.

The intelligence probes had paid off handsomely, but the yield was also very troubling to this dedicated warrior.

Tendrils of the Mafia cancer were woven throughout the fabric of this great little city's business and social communities. The in-growth

114

was still tenuous, however, and the encroachment had not yet reached the cannibalistic stage.

But Mack Bolan knew his enemy.

And he had learned quite a bit, in a relatively short time, about the city of San Diego.

And, yeah, this was one city he could not avoid.

Some of the area's most solid citizens had been trekking to the tar pits of licensed greed—in many cases, perhaps, unaware that a band of cannibals were lurking there in the shadows, patiently awaiting the opportunity to ensnare them there and devour them—that some were already being eaten.

A sober and troubled electronics expert stored his surveillance tapes in a fireproof box and turned a thoughtful frown to his friend, the Executioner.

"So now what?" he asked, sighing.

"So now the siege is ended," Bolan replied quietly.

"You mean we pack up and walk away," Blancanales said.

"No. We storm the city."

"Oh, well. . . ." The Politician scratched his nose, glanced at Schwarz, and said, "What's the first target?"

"The tar pits," Bolan told them.

"The tar pits?"

"Yeah." Bolan was buckling into his AutoMag.

"You mean like the LaBrea tar pits, up in L.A.?"

"Something like that," Bolan said. "Only these are invisible."

Schwarz and Blancanales exchanged puzzled glances. They were accustomed to Bolan's sometimes cryptic utterances, but this one left them blank.

"They've dug bones of woolly mammoths and I think dinosaurs out of LaBrea," Schwarz commented.

"We're after bigger game than that," the Executioner assured his crew.

"It's still a rescue mission?" Blancanales wanted to know.

"That," Bolan replied, "is exactly what it is."

13: THE LINK

She was young, beautiful, married to one of San Diego's most illustrious citizens, and—according to her own immodest claim in a telephone conversation with Lisa Winters—she had "balled every hood in this town . . . and a few over in Mexico."

Her hair was shades of red and hung in a full drop to a point just below her shoulders. The eyes were emerald-hued, but lacked sparkle. The body was long and shapely with soft curves that flowed one into the other beneath velvet-textured skin. A true redhead, the sun apparently was not kind to her; she was glistening and greasy with protective oils and lotions. She wore a micro-bikini which did not quite conceal the fringes of the silky growth of hair at the base of her soft little tummy.

She was topless—one of those who could get away with it admirably.

With all that, if Bolan had ever seen a truly turned-off young woman, then this was the one.

She was sprawled upon her back on a large beach towel, head and shoulders supported by a plastic pillow, staring at him with something less than curiosity. A large Doberman, identical to the dogs at the Winters place, sat faithfully at her feet and regarded Bolan with that same detachment.

Needlessly, it seemed, she commanded the dog, "Thunder, stay." Then she told the intruder, "This is a private beach."

Bolan replied, "I know."

Except for the hat, he was dressed in the seagoing togs he'd acquired for the hit on *Danger's Folly*. The AutoMag was snugged into a shoulder holster beneath his left arm. The big piece made a noticeable bulge in his jacket, but this was the desired effect.

She was looking him over with a shade of interest now.

"You can be prosecuted for trespassing," Maxwell Thornton's wife informed the Executioner.

He said, "I'll risk it."

She sat up, sending the undraped chest a'jiggling, and leaned forward to grab a handful of the dog's coat. "Thunder is my bodyguard," she declared in that same listless tone. "A word from me and he'll be at your throat."

Beneath that turned-off exterior, the girl was frightened. Bolan knew this by the way the dog was beginning to tense and strain. A good dog could sense its owner's concealed emotions.

He told her, "Thunder must be a real comfort. Too bad."

The dog was off his fanny now, legs beneath him in a low crouch, lips curling upward to show this intruder how impressive his fangs were.

After a brief silence, the girl asked, "What's too bad?"

"Too bad that Howlie couldn't get the same sense of security from Thunder's brothers."

That one penetrated, immediately.

She let go of the Doberman and cried, "Thunder, *hit!*"

The big fellow's trained reaction was instantaneous and dramatic. The soft sand gave him a little trouble, but just a little, and he left the ground with all four feet airborne, snarling into the conditioned-response attack, the great mouth fully open and grinding into that contact with human flesh.

It is impossible to depict a true guard-dog attack in one of those staged presentations for movies or television. The Hollywood dogs are trained to simulate an attack and there is no way to fake the actual fury and viciousness of a true guard-dog response to a *kill* command.

These impressive fellows do not passively wrestle about with their jaws clamped lightly around a guy's forearm. They *explode* into a writhing juggernaut of fury unleashed, slashing and ripping with fang and claw, and it is a rare man who can bare-handedly stand up to such an assault.

Mack Bolan was a rare man.

He had read the attack, and he'd been waiting for it. His jump-off was synchronized with that

119

of the dog as he pivoted inside and under the scrambling leap. He popped him in the throat with everything he could put behind a balled fist and rammed a knee into the belly as the Doberman fell back onto his hind legs.

It was a matter of an irresistible force meeting an immovable object, with the immovable object getting the best shots in.

The Doberman's legs buckled. The big head drooped toward the sand as he alternately coughed and retched, struggling to draw air with his temporarily paralyzed respiratory system.

He was all out of fight, for the moment.

Bolan sprung the AutoMag and aimed it at the Doberman's head. "Call him off," he warned the woman.

It had all occurred so quickly that the woman's hand was still poised in the air where she had released the dog. Those emerald eyes did not so much as flicker as she issued the soft command. "Thunder, break."

The monster-dog seemed grateful to be relieved of his responsibilities. He crawled toward the woman, whining and still fighting for breath.

Bolan sheathed the AutoMag and knelt beside the dog to rub his throat and massage the quivering ribcage.

Something was coming alive in Marsha Thornton's dead eyes as she watched the tall man with the impassive face stroke the suffering animal. She murmured, "I wouldn't believe that if I hadn't seen it. I was assured that Thunder would protect me from a grizzly bear."

Bolan said, "He would."

His jacket was ripped and he was bleeding slightly from a fang-graze on his hand.

The woman rolled onto her knees and stood up. "Come on up to the house," she suggested. "I'll put something on that cut."

The Doberman was licking the fingers which had defeated him, and Bolan was thinking what a shame it was to misuse a dog this way. Man's oldest friend in the animal world, converted to a living robot, programmed to kill upon command.

The dog and Mack Bolan had a great deal in common—Bolan realized that. He'd pondered the question after a run-in with a couple of German Shepherds during the New York battle. And he'd decided then that there *was* a difference—subtle but important—between himself and the killer dog.

The dogs killed because they were conditioned to accept a command to do so. In a dog's world, it was a sort of a *morality* to be obedient to his master's desires. Actually, Bolan knew, guard-dogs killed because *they had to kill*. There was no mental or moral alternative.

Bolan did not *have* to kill.

He killed *because he could*—and because, like the dogs, there was no mental or moral alternative.

So, yeah, he had a lot in common with the Doberman—but with a difference. A very important difference.

He pushed the thing from his mind and followed Marsha Thornton to her beach house, the Doberman huffing along at his side.

It seemed that he had made a conquest.

If all went well, he would very soon make another.

While Bolan cultivated the distaff side of the House of Thornton, Schwarz and Blancanales invaded an impressively modern skyscraper in downtown San Diego for a call upon the master himself.

The solid oak door was marked GOLDEN WEST DIVERSITIES, INC. and the suite of offices on the other side of it were strictly gilt-edged, redolent with the sweet smell of success.

Among the diversified interests of Maxwell Thornton was petroleum, real estate, electronics, agriculture, and transportation. He had also been very active in politics, as a behind-the-scenes power in local, state, and national campaigns.

Blancanales had donned a pale blue nylon suit with coordinated accessories—the collar of the shirt with exaggerated dimensions, the tie immaculately knotted, powder-blue hat low over the eyes—altogether a splendiferous image, and altogether the perfect picture of a *Mafioso* in full dress.

Schwarz wore old-fashioned pleated slacks, sport shirt with loose tie, checkered sports coat, no hat. He looked like a cross between a Tijuana pimp and an Agua Caliente racetrack tout.

Both images had been meticulously contrived.

The receptionist stared at them for a moment, then announced, "I'm sorry, Mr. Thornton is in conference."

"You'd better get him outta there, honey," Blancanales growled in his best Brooklynese.

Schwarz had spun the woman's appointments book around and was studying it.

Blancanales nudged the flustered receptionist

again with, "Hop, *now!*—go tell the man we're here."

"I-I'll see if he's back in his office," the girl replied, thoroughly intimidated now. She depressed a button on her desk intercom and said, "Mr. Thornton—two gentlemen to see you. It appears urgent. They—I think you should."

A tired voice sighed back, "Do the gentlemen have names, Janie?"

Schwarz brushed the receptionist's hand aside and held the intercom button himself as he replied, "Yeh, but you wouldn't want 'em shouted around this joint, Thornton."

"Come on in," was the quick response.

The girl showed them the way. Blancanales patted her shoulder as he brushed past her and into the private office of Maxwell Thornton.

The entire outside wall was glass, and there was a fair-sized balcony beyond that with potted trees and other growing things. The city was spread out there for inspection in a most impressive view.

The man sat at a kidney-shaped desk with probably fifty to sixty square feet of surface on top which supported nothing except a telephone, an intercom box, and an open fifth of Haig & Haig.

The guy was drinking the Scotch from a water glass, undiluted.

He didn't look the part of millionaire, civic light, city father. He looked like a guy who'd just stepped down from a hot bulldozer to hurry into a hand-tailored suit which still somehow didn't quite fit. A tall man, lanky, sort of gangly and rawboned, well past fifty.

The voice fit the rest of him as he waved his

visitors to chairs and told them, "Well, I guess the shit has hit the fan, hasn't it?"

Schwarz picked up the bottle of Scotch and sat down. Blancanales remained standing. He said, "Bolan's in town."

Thornton sighed, sipped at his drink, then said, "I know it."

"Gettin' loaded ain't gonna help."

"Get fucked," Thornton growled. "Bennie send you? What's he want me to do, lead a vigilante army?"

"Bennie don't send *us*," Schwarz informed him.

The gray steel eyes came up in a quick flash. "New York? You're from New York?"

Blancanales jerked his head in a nod and ambled to the window.

"Who are you?"

Schwarz replied. "The boss is Harry DiCavoli. I'm Jack Santo. You're in trouble, Thornton."

The millionaire grunted and said, "I was born in trouble. I suppose you heard about Howlie Winters."

"We heard," Blancanales spoke up, from the window. "We wanta talk to you about that, Thornton."

"You people squeezed him too damn hard!" the man declared angrily. "I told you he wouldn't hold still for that."

"You told *me* nothing," Blancanales/DiCavoli replied.

"I told Bennie, and I urged him to relay the advice to New York. Look . . . Winters was a square. A guy like that will dabble in the shit pile, but he won't take a bath in it. I told you this whole thing was too much for him to swill."

"I guess you better speak for yourself, man," Blancanales said.

"What do you mean? Look. . . ." The guy was getting hotter by the minute. He pushed back his chair and lifted himself to his full height, and it was an impressive one. He was waving his arms as he spoke. "I had to swim in shit to get where I am. I'll never deny that, except in a court of law. I've had the *course*, buddy. I've been there and back, several times. You goddam ghetto street-corner lawyers didn't invent the game, and you don't play it very well. The only edge you've got is that you play it *rougher* than most. Well, get fucked, will you please? I've had it up to the throat with you, *all* of you."

Blancanales muttered, "You want me to go back East and tell 'em that?"

The guy had moved away from the desk. He was standing spread-legged, coat gaping open, hands thrust into hip pockets, glowering at the man at the window. His eyes dropped, slowly, and his voice was dying away as he replied, "No . . . I guess I don't want you to do that."

"That's just what we come to find out."

"I can take the heat, if that's what's worrying you."

Schwarz had risen from his chair and edged his backside onto the desk. With Thornton engrossed in the confrontation with eastern authority, he was quietly and swiftly taking the telephone apart.

"That ain't all," Blancanales was saying. "We been waiting long enough for this deal. Now with Winters out of the picture, we have to wonder. . . ."

"Don't worry, you'll get your stuff. With or

125

without Winters. But listen—what's the name—DiCavoli?—listen, DiCavoli, this is no dime-store radio, you know. We're into defense security violation when we start messing around with this kind of gear."

Schwarz's ears perked up at that. His work at the telephone was finished. He moved toward the other men and joined the conversation. "That's right, Harry. It's not dime-store stuff."

Blancanales quickly picked up the play. "A radio's a radio," he sniffed. "What's such a big deal?"

Thornton coldly returned Schwarz's gaze as he replied to the other *"Mafioso."* "An L-band feeder horn is a *hell* of a big deal when you start stealing them from the military."

"Well we gotta know," Blancanales pushed on. "Are you going to deliver or aren't you?"

"Of course I'm going to deliver! But, my God, you don't just muscle your way into—"

"It's heavy stuff, Harry," Schwarz helpfully butted in. He was probing, now—feeling his way. At the same time, he was establishing a sympathetic relationship with the harried millionaire who'd lingered too long near the tar pit. "You can't pick up a feeder horn at the supermarket, y'know. This stuff is heavy, I mean *heavy*. What is it, Max —about six hundred megs?"

Thornton inclined his head in a deliberate nod. He was giving Schwarz a respectful examination now, wondering, pondering the enigma of a Tijuana pimp who spoke with an understanding of sophisticated communications gear.

Schwarz was "explaining" to Blancanales/DiCavoli. "Y'see, these data links, you pencil-beam into a dish antenna up in the L-band, around six hundred megacycles. It's like a beam of light, only you don't *see* it. You don't get no side lobes off the pulse envelopes, so there ain't much danger of the FCC or somebody latching onto you. Right, Max?"

Thornton again nodded his head. "It's fool-proof," he murmured.

"And the stuff is hard to come by," Schwarz went on explaining. "You don't just walk up and ask a government contractor to make you one. You'd have the FCC all over your ass the second you tried to put it on the air—and in no time you'd have feds swarming all over your operation. What Max is saying is simply this: we gotta be patient while he carves one out of a contract. Right, Max?"

Thornton quietly replied, "Yes. Just like the last one."

"I guess I wasn't in on that one," Blancanales declared innocently.

"Just who are you people?" Thornton asked, his voice barely audible.

"We came with the man," Blancanales replied, dropping the street accent.

"What man?" Thornton asked wearily.

"Bolan," Schwarz said, soberly studying their victim.

The guy walked jerkily back to his desk and sat down. He poured several fingers of Haig & Haig into his glass and belted it, then wiped his lips with the back of his hand.

"I've been there and back," he declared quietly. "But I sure talked myself into this one, didn't I?"

"Keep trying," Blancanales suggested. "Maybe you'll talk your way *out* of something."

"You're in deep shit, Max," Schwarz said gently.

The guy was trapped, and he knew it. He studied his empty glass for a moment, then raised resigned eyes to Gadgets Schwarz. "I was born in shit," he murmured.

"So now you got a chance to wipe yourself," Schwarz told him. "How about it?"

"Full redemption, huh?"

"We can't promise that."

"All right," the self-made millionaire muttered. "Pass the toilet paper."

Lancers
Vinho Branco
means
white wine.

Who knows
what it will
mean to
you.

IMPORTED
LANCERS.
Vinho Branco
A WHITE DINNER WINE

LANCERS® VINHO BRANCO. WHITE DINNER WINE.
SOLE IMPORTERS. ©1972, HEUBLEIN, INC., HARTFORD, CT.

Give your cold to Contac.
Get early cold care.

14: TAR

Bolan's interrogation of Marsha Thornton was revealing very little in the nature of direct intelligence, but she was filling in quite a bit of background insight into the San Diego situation.

"Max is quite a bit older than I am, you know," she told Bolan in that curious turned-off voice. "I wouldn't mind that. I mean, I guess I love him. He's a perfect husband . . . in every way but one. Gives me everything I want. Except himself. He . . . can't. So I have to go find that somewhere else."

"And Max just turns his head, eh."

"Yes. He understands. He just asks that I be . . . discreet. I guess I've caused him a lot of embarrassment, just the same."

"It figures," Bolan told her.

"Yes. Well, you'd have to know my husband to

understand how *gross* all this could be for him.
I mean, a man like him. Well . . . I have no apologies to make to anyone, except to Max I guess, and
he won't let me. He simply understands. I've had
a hunger ever since my boobs starting budding,
Mr. Bolan. I can't turn it off. Don't get the wrong
idea. I'm no nympho. But when I'm hungry, I'm
hungry."

Bolan murmured, "I can understand that." He
was getting a bit of an itch, himself.

"You probably think I'm a nympho," she said,
deadpanning a sidewise gaze in his direction. He
got very few direct looks from this one. "It's okay,
you may as well think it. Everybody else does.
I've been in analysis. My analyst says I am definitely *not* a nympho."

Bolan said, "Okay."

"I hated those hoods. They just kept hanging
around Max. Oh, they never came through the
front door . . . don't worry. But they were always
around, always popping up, always underfoot.
We'd go out to dinner, and there they'd be. We'd
go to a club, and there they'd be." She sighed, a
long painful effort. "I guess I figured they may
as well be in the bedroom, too. Instant manpower."

Bolan told her, "You don't have to get into this
if you'd rather not. I had the Winters telephone
tapped. I heard your conversation with Lisa this
morning."

That revelation drew not so much as a blink of
the eyes. "Lisa's a good kid. We're about the same
age, you know. Body age, not soul age. God, my
soul must be a million years old."

Bolan could almost believe it.

"I guess, really, I was trying to punish Max by

balling his underworld pals. I guess I was getting back at him."

"Humiliating him," Bolan suggested.

"That's what my analyst says. He calls it soiling myself in my husband's own dirt pile. Oh . . . it's humiliated him, all right. But as soon as I realized it, I broke it off. You know, I cut out." The deadened eyes traveled to the dog. "That's when I got Thunder. Those hoods wouldn't take no as an answer, not from me. They'd just walk in and grab me by the ass, throw me a quick one, and walk out laughing. Boy. Talk about humiliation. Well, that was six months ago. Lisa was taking lessons at this kennels out on Cabrillo Highway, learning to handle the dogs. I decided to take the training with her, and I ended up with old Thunder here."

She surprised Bolan with a girlish giggle. "Today was the first time I ever ordered him to attack and wow, did you see him getting with it!"

He growled, "Yeah, I saw it."

"I'm really glad he didn't hurt you. You're a nice man, so far I guess. But I had to have Thunder, see. I found out those hoods were passing me around between them, giggling and snickering about me, and I'm sure it all got back to Max. His nympho wife."

The girl shivered and suddenly stood up. She was still clad only in the micro-bikini, bottom only, nothing else. She crossed her arms over the bare chest and walked out onto the sun deck. Thunder trotted along after her.

Bolan drifted out there, also. He stood behind her and gazed over her head at the impossibly blue Pacific with its foaming leading edges rolling onto the beach just below them.

It all seemed, suddenly, totally unreal.

These human moments stole up on a guy, surprising him in the midst of combat, reminding him of his mortality, his humanness.

At this moment, Mack Bolan felt entirely human.

He'd come to this town to blitz it, to wade through blood if necessary, to shake the rats out of their nests. He had not come here for a human experience.

But here he was in the presence of a lovely young woman, sharing her nakedness of body and soul.

He told her, very gently, "Look, Marsha . . . all the perfect people are in heaven."

She tilted the shiny red head over her shoulder and smiled at him. Life was forming somewhere back there behind those glazed eyes.

Perhaps, he thought, she was having a human experience also. She asked him, the smile turning sober, "Do you have to kill my husband?"

He replied honestly. "At this point, I don't know. What can you tell me to help my decision?"

She shrugged, delicately. "I just wish you wouldn't. Maybe it's not too late. What can I tell you about Max? I can tell you how he likes his eggs, that he hates pretension and that he loves me very very much . . . even at my worst. Is that enough to get him off?"

Bolan did not reply.

She shivered again and tightened the hold on her chest. "He's not like them, Mr. Bolan. Oh . . . in his own way, he may be worse than them. More crooked, I mean. He'll admit that he's a crook, it's how he made his fortune. He's a real wheeler-dealer and he's kind of proud of it. But he's not like *them*." She shuddered. Her voice became tiny as she added, "He just can't get *loose* from them."

"What's their hold?" he asked her.

"Me, for one thing. But they already had him hog-tied before I came along."

"You how?"

"Oh, this rotten business. Do you know a man called Tony Danger?"

Bolan nodded.

"I went to a party on his yacht. A cruise to Ensenada. Two other girls. Two of Tony's hoods. We . . . partied. While Tony took motion pictures of it. I was so stoned on grass, I. . . ."

Bolan said, "Never mind, I know the routine."

"Yes, well, he showed Max some stills from that film. In *my* presence. Can you beat that? Max didn't say a word, didn't bat an eyelash. Tony told him the negatives were in New York. That they'd stay there in a special file. Just in case Max felt like busting out his britches, as Tony put it. Well, as rotten as I am, I guess Max would do anything to keep them from circulating something like that. I guess. . . ."

Bolan muttered, "Maybe Max is making pilgrimages to the soiling grounds, himself."

She stared at him for a moment then said, "I hadn't thought of that. You mean maybe he's punishing himself for his inadequacy?"

Bolan shrugged. "I'm no psychologist. But it's a thought."

"Yes, isn't it," she agreed.

There was a definite luster in the girl's eyes now.

133

Bolan didn't want to spoil it, but he had to ask her. "Was Lisa Winters in that party—the boat trip to Ensenada?"

She wet her lips and told him, "Well, you'd have to ask her about that."

He replied, "Okay. I will."

She swiveled about and wrapped her arms about Bolan's neck in one swift motion, kissed him lightly on the mouth, then released him.

"Five minutes ago," she said breathlessly, "I was starved half to death. And hating myself for it. I'm not hungry now. You'd better go while you can."

"I'll want a rain check on about an hour of your time, at my demand," he told her. "And it has nothing to do with hunger."

"You've got it," she assured him. "Now split, before my monster awakens."

Bolan believed her.

And he split.

But his monster had already awakened, and he was hungry as hell.

"Howlie had been crumbling for months," Blancanales reported. "They got into him on little stuff, nickle and dime jazz, during his GHQ stint at Saigon. I guess he was a little bitter over the deal he got, you know, and he was ripe for the approach. You know how a guy like Howlin' Harlan must have felt at a *logistics* desk, God's sake."

"Yeah," Bolan agreed.

"Anyway, he was in a position to set them up for dumping contraband into the PX and service club circuits. Thornton was dragged into it from this end, via his transportation outfits. He even hijacked some of his own trucks and collected insurance on the loss. Anyway, he was able to provide bonafide shipping orders and such for the loot and he even had a couple of freighters in the play. They were running everything from shaving lotion to hootch. According to Thornton, Southeast Asia, for awhile there, was the prime dumping grounds for the hijack rings."

"Cute," Bolan commented.

"Yeh. When these guys do something, they do it big, don't they. Well, according to Thornton, he wasn't getting that much out of it. He figured the risk exceeded the profits, most of which was going to the mob anyway. But they had it into him, and he had to go along."

"What were you saying about Howlie?" Bolan reminded him.

"Well, he was nickle-and-diming it during his last few months at Saigon. After his retirement, Thornton helped him set up here. Thornton swears it and I don't know why he'd want to lie about it now . . . Howlie didn't know what he was getting into, not at first. Oh sure, he knew he was selling his influence at the Pentagon. I guess they all do it, most of these retired officers. Why not? It's legal, right? And it's about the only way they can make a military career pay off when things have gone sour for them. Who needs a guy who has spent his whole life deploying troops around a battlefield, right?"

"Go on," Bolan prodded.

Schwarz took it from there. "You know what a feeder horn is, Sarge? It's part of a radio transmission system, sort of like microwave but still operating at radio frequencies. It puts out a controlled emission that's beamed like a spotlight, only it's tighter than any spotlight. It's line-of-sight stuff. The other end of the system uses a dish-antenna for receiving, and you have to shoot directly into the dish or there's no reception."

"Radio point-blank," Bolan commented. "We had them in 'Nam."

"Right. Data links for radar, electronic counter-measures."

"Ultra-sophisticated," Blancanales put in.

"Absolutely," Schwarz agreed. "I have no idea what a rig like that costs, but you can bet it's mighty heavy. You can set them up for mobile use, and that gets even costlier. Besides that, if you're going to own a system like that then you've got to have people who know how to operate and maintain it. Now why. . . ." He paused, grinned, and swiped at his nose with a balled fist. "Why would you think an outfit like the Mafia would want a million-dollar toy like that?"

Bolan showed the electronics expert a sober smile and said, "Data link, right?"

"Right."

"With Agua Caliente just a few miles across the border."

Schwarz looked disappointed. Bolan had spoiled his punch line. "That's it," he said. "The track down there has a complete foreign book betting service for tracks all over the world. These dummies are trying to set up a foolproof link between Mexico and Vegas. At mountain peak to mountain peak line-of-sight, do you know how many feeder-horn relays they'd have to have?"

Bolan commented, "They think big, Gadgets."
He shrugged his shoulders. "And if it's costing
them nothing...."

"Well yeah, but God what they have to go
through to *get* the stuff. That's what finally stuck
in Howlie's craw. He helped them get two systems
already, without even realizing what he was doing. Then he stumbled onto it and tried to freeze
them out. It was a neat racket and I'd like to meet
the guy who thought it up. Thornton's electronics
subsidiary is subbing on a military contract for
a whole bunch of these rigs, complete systems.
Thornton supplies various components used in
the final assembly. One of Howlie's companies had
the final inspection and quality assurance contract *for the military*. Through quality rejects and
a lot of juggling, they managed to piecemeal-out
enough rejected components to assemble two complete systems. They've got them holed up somewhere right now, Thornton swears he doesn't
know where, until they get enough to complete the
link to Vegas. But God, it was a sweet idea. I
guess they marked the QC rejects as salvage, can-
celled-out the serial numbers, and buried all the
records of the final transactions."

"Or burned them," Bolan said. He was remem-
bering a thick stack of ashes in the Winters fireplace. "Could those be the papers Lisa Winters
was yelling about?"

"It's beginning to make sense," Blancanales
said thoughtfully. "Howlie was a poor sap, a dupe.
He dug up the records and took them home . . .
maybe to study them and confirm his suspicions.
Once he knew, he told them to go to hell."

"He would do that," Schwarz said musingly.

"He'd have to have an edge on them somewhere," Bolan pointed out. "And his edge was the records. He could expose the whole scheme by publicly producing those records."

"Mexican stand-off," Blancanales said. "He'd also be incriminating himself. So he couldn't just haul off and let fire. But . . . as long as he had those papers. . . ."

"Right," Bolan agreed. "So why would he burn them? He had the boys over a barrel."

"Maybe he just couldn't keep them there," Schwarz said quietly.

"It's why he sent for Able Team," Blancanales decided.

"Too late," Schwarz murmured.

"Too late for the living," Bolan told them, ice creeping into his voice. "But not too late for the dead. Come on. We're moving out."

"Where to?" the Politician inquired.

"*You*, to see a young lady. Concerning a stack of papers and *why* they were burned."

"Wait'll I comb my hair," Blancanales said, grinning.

Bolan stabbed Gadgets Schwarz with his eyes. "You've got the cold job," he warned him. "Find that stolen gear."

Schwarz's eyelids fluttered rapidly, but all he had to say about the assignment was, "Okay. So I'll bundle up good."

Bolan did not share the secret with his buddies, but he had saved the really cold job for himself.

It was time to spread the tar around.

He had to roust Tony Danger.

Even if it meant rousting him from a jail cell.

He did not know it at that moment, but a jail cell was precisely where he'd have to go to nail the guy.

15: COLD PLAY

It was getting dark out when Carl Lyons and John Tatum decamped from the Captain's office, headed toward a quick meal and a few casual moments of relaxation before facing the long night ahead.

It had been a rough day of dreary police work—interrogations, questioning of witnesses, seemingly endless conferences with city and county officials, and finally the big Mafia roundup of outraged and bitterly complaining local honchos.

That last had been the worst, in Tatum's book. The mob had plenty of clout in the area, at every court level, and it had been damn tough just getting an overnight hold on the swaggering bastards without specific charges to book them on.

A legal eagle in the D.A.'s office had finally come up with one of those old "public good" statutes which was at least firm enough to base an argument upon until morning.

Maybe that would save the night, anyway.

Tatum paused at the duty desk to sign himself out, and he told the young cop from L.A., "I don't know, maybe Braddock is right and this *is* the best way to cope with the problem. Maybe we can just stalemate the guy out of town. It may be an ounce of prevention, but it sure isn't good police work, not in my book."

"The important thing is to hold down the fireworks," Lyons remarked. "Bolan isn't all that big and bad. And I guess he figures there's always a next time. He'll play the odds, that's for sure. For him, the numbers say *don't push it—another time is coming.*"

"It'd better not," Tatum replied grimly. "One more killing and this town will blow sky high. God, the *pressure*. Did you feel it in there?"

"I felt it," Lyons admitted.

"And the press hasn't even got ahold of it yet." The Captain glanced at the clock above the duty desk. "That is, for another five minutes. I don't know how the word gets around, but they tell me the city-hall phones have been burning all afternoon."

"Concerned citizens," Lyons suggested wryly.

"Yeah, very *important* concerned citizens."

"That should tell you something."

"It tells me plenty. But what the hell can I prove?"

Lyons shrugged. The Captain finished signing-out and they went on along the corridor toward the vehicle area.

A tall patrolman in an immaculate uniform,

141

sporting a thinline mustache, swung in from a side corridor, nodded his head cordially at Lyons, and went on by.

The sergeant from L.A. grunted and asked the San Diego homicide chief, "You allowing face hair down here now?"

"Had to," Tatum said grumpily. "They got a constitutional right . . . and they also got a damn good union. What the hell. So long as it's not too far out, what's the harm? You gotta sway with the times, I guess. We're not still running around in Toonerville Cop uniforms, are we."

Lyons grinned. "No, but the Toonervilles wore face hair."

"So, change is sometimes a healthy thing . . . even in a town like San Diego."

"That's right," Lyons agreed. He stepped outside and took a deep breath. "You've got a sweet town here, Cap'n."

"Thanks."

They walked to the Captain's personal vehicle. Lyons slid in beside Tatum and told him, "Maybe you shouldn't feel so bad about a Bolan visit. The guy has a way of clearing the air, making things even sweeter."

"I'll pretend you didn't say that," Tatum replied gruffly.

Lyons chuckled. "I told you I owed the guy my life. I didn't tell you I owe him *twice*. You heard about the deal on Charlie Rickert, I guess."

"Rotten apple," the Captain rasped.

"Sure, but we may have never known if it hadn't been for Bolan. He tipped us about the guy. I couldn't believe it at first. You know what they called Rickert . . . the twenty-four-hour cop. He

142

was a twelve-hour-cop and a twenty-four-hour *Mafioso*. This next bit never got in the book, so don't blow it. Rickert was all set to blast me into the next world. Bolan didn't have to make the save . . . it could have turned sour on him real easy. But he did."

"And here you are," Tatum remarked quietly.

"Then there was Las Vegas. I was up there on special assignment with a federal strike force. Undercover job. I dummied it, and the boys tumbled to me. Beat the living shit out of me. They were hauling me to the desert to bury me alive when Bolan turned up. The guy challenged a motor convoy. Single handed. Blasted them to kingdom-come, right in the shadow of their fortress, then slipped me out of there with half of the Nevada mob on his ass. And I couldn't even *walk*."

Tatum sighed heavily and said, "Hey, cut it out. I've heard all the songs about the guy. I still have a job to do."

"Sure, that's the way I feel," Lyons said. "Bolan knows it, too. Any other way and I don't think he'd respect me. He's that kind of guy. Hard-nosed as hell when it comes to duty and ethics. I'll tell you one thing, Cap'n. I'm sure glad he doesn't shoot at cops."

"I've heard that one, too," Tatum growled.

"Believe it."

The Captain relented, grinning, and declared, "Some cops I've seen, maybe he *should* go after them."

Lyons sat bolt upright in the seat and smacked a hand against his forehead. "That cop!" he yelled.

"*What* cop?"

143

"The dude with the mustache. Hell oh hell, John, it was *him!*"

"Him what? What's the matter with you?"

"It was *Bolan!* Walking around your station in a *uniform!*"

"Aw bullshit," Tatum snarled. "What would Bolan be doing . . . ?"

He pulled the car to the curb with a screech of tires and lunged toward his radio microphone.

"I thought you knew the fucking guy so personally," he yelled at Lyons.

"Aw hell, you never get that much of a look at the clever bastard, John. He's a *genius* at this sort of thing, and I'm telling you *he's in your station house!*"

"For *what?*"

"What the hell do you think for what? Where are all the boys tonight, John?"

Tatum's hand was frozen around the microphone. He squawked, "Well *Jesus Christ!* We'll be the laughing stock of . . . !"

He flung the microphone down and doubled back in a screeching U-turn, burning rubber toward the possibly most disgraceful discovery in twenty-six years of hard-nosed police work.

The Executioner, for God's sake! Making a hit on the San Diego jail!

Bolan had been required to hang around the locker room for only about ten minutes before spotting the size and type of guy he was waiting for—a young patrolman going off duty and changing into civvies.

And it had been a simple task, after the cop departed, to pick the lock and borrow the uniform. It was a good fit. He even took the time to use the guy's brush to get rid of a bit of lint here and there. He wanted to look sharp.

He left a marksman's medal and three fifty-dollar bills on a shelf in the locker, quickly applied a false mustache to his upper lip, and went out of there.

He was only a few steps out of the locker room when he rounded a corner, practically colliding with Carl Lyons and another detective.

And that was a bad moment for the Executioner.

Of all the cops in the world he didn't need to bump into at a time like this, Lyons was first. He was one of the few men living who'd had intimate opportunities to get to know Bolan's new face.

The bogus cop smiled faintly at his old friend of past campaigns, tucked his chin down in what he hoped would pass as a friendly nod and brazened on past.

He kept expecting a cry of alarm—was mentally preparing himself for it and looking for a way out—but when he reached the duty desk and risked a glance over his shoulder, Lyons and the other cop were nowhere in view.

The building was crowded and confused, lots of in-and-out traffic, standing-around traffic, and just plain officious bustling—noise level about equal to a concert by the Rolling Stones.

Bolan stepped up to the desk and told the sergeant, "Jail pass."

The guy glanced at the badge on Bolan's chest

and reached for a paper form. "Courts?" he asked disinterestedly.

Bolan replied, "Prosecutor's office."

The cop grunted and shoved the pass at him.

Cold, yeah.

Siberian shivery cold.

But . . . so far, so good.

He wandered around from there until he found the detention section. The jail warden's desk was flanked by a group of irritable-looking and noisy men carrying briefcases.

Bolan had an idea who they were.

He pushed through them and leaned across the desk to speak in low tones to the cop on duty there. He showed him the pass and told him, "D.A. wants one of your VIPs over in interrogation." He flicked his eyes significantly toward the group of civilians. "Let's not mention any names."

He was going through the booking records as he spoke. He found the card he wanted and pushed it at the duty warden. "This one. We won't want to bring him through here."

The cop nodded his head, understanding. He jotted something on Bolan's pass and told him, "Take him out the back. I'll call down and clear it for you."

The man from blood nodded and went on, into the cell block, showing his pass and picking up an escort there, past the tank and along a musty row of cells.

The escort pulled up at a door about halfway along, turned a key in the lock, and told the Executioner, "Here's your man."

It sure was.

Tony Danger sauntered out, a nasty smile

straining at his face. "Told you peasants I wouldn't be here for supper," he gloated.

Bolan wordlessly signed a receipt for the prisoner, then spun him around and shoved him toward the rear of the building.

"Watch that!" Tony Danger snarled. "I'll have your fuckin' badge!"

Bolan winked at the escort and left him standing there at the cell door as he hustled the prisoner toward the rear exit. He signed another receipt there and took his man along a short corridor and outside to the vehicle area.

"What is this?" the *Mafioso* asked suspiciously, his head jerking about in an awareness of the unusual procedure as Bolan dragged him to a car and opened the door.

Bolan spoke for the first time since the initial encounter. "Don't argue, Mr. Danger. Just get in the damn car, please sir."

"What? Are you nuts? A jailbreak? Hey—my lawyers will—"

"You can't stop Bolan with a writ, Mr. Danger." The tall man in the police uniform shoved the protesting *caporegime* into the seat and slammed the door, then went quickly around to the driver's side and climbed in.

"What are you saying?" Tony Danger demanded, all but frothing at the mouth in a mixture of bewilderment and indignant anger. "The guy wouldn't have the nerve to bust in there after anybody!"

Bolan had the car moving. He nearly collided with another vehicle that came screeching into the parking lot, horn blaring. The other car whipped away just in time to avoid the collision.

Bolan caught a glimpse of a tortured face behind the wheel of that vehicle and—beside it—a flashing impression of the amused yet somber features of the all-cop from L.A., Carl Lyons.

Then he was into the street, accelerating with everything the Ferrari had. It became obvious quickly that there was no pursuit so he eased off and angled a glance toward his unhappy passenger.

"What did you say, Tony?" he asked frigidly.

"I said the guy wouldn't have the nerve to. . . ."

The sounds just gurgled away and the little *Mafioso* was turning to stone, his mouth agape, staring with a horrifying awakening at the freeze-dried face of the big guy behind the wheel.

"Don't lose your voice now, Tony," Bolan advised him. "It's the only thing you've got between life and death."

At that, it was a hell of a lot more than the Executioner could have had going for him, back at San Diego jail.

Cold, yeah.

It was what his game was made of.

Cold blood.

16: OFF THE NUMBERS

They had cleared the area of all but official personnel and the morgue-like silence in that big hall was being well-resonated by the quivering-with-rage voice of Captain John Tatum.

He was leaning forward with both big hands splayed out across the jail warden's desk, his face thrust to within an inch of the other poor guy's as he shouted, "Yes, I said *kidnap!* You let Mack Bolan stroll in here and *kidnap* one of your prisoners!"

The officer was desperately trying to get the homicide chief to consider two slips of paper which he was holding between trembling fingers. He spluttered, "Hell, Cap'n, he signed the receipts."

Tatum leaned back with a defeated sigh. There was nothing to be gained by badgering the poor

bastard, the sigh seemed to say. In a voice subdued and embittered, he told the duty warden,
"Okay, Tom. You go tell the watch captain not to
worry, that you've got signed receipts for the
missing prisoner. You can paste them to his forehead when they bring him back . . . to the
morgue."

The desk cop muttered, "Hell, it was just cut
and dried routine. How was I to know? I can't
personally recognize every officer on this force.
Hell, we got—"

"I know the strength of our force," Tatum
rasped. "Now you listen. You're on duty until the
chief himself says otherwise. Got that? You don't
go home, you don't even go to the pot. You see
nobody and you talk to nobody who isn't toting a
badge, and even then it'd better be somebody you
know by sight. Got that?"

The guy nodded his head in miserable understanding.

Carl Lyons had been watching the performance
from the safe background. Tatum turned to him
and growled, "What were you telling me about
Bolan playing the odds? Some odds. This is the
Goddamnedest most outrageous grandstand play
I ever heard of."

Lyons shrugged and dropped his eyes in com-
miseration for the other man's torment. Often-
times, he realized, the flesh beneath those tough
old police hides was painfully sensitive. He said,
"I forgot to tell you. The guy sometimes makes
his own odds. I don't know what to say, John. I
just don't know."

"Well I've got to keep the wraps on this bullshit
as long as I can. Maybe something will . . . hell,

this is a nightmare. I don't believe it. How can I tell them—those lawyers, the D.A., the court—how do I tell them a *public good* prisoner has been kidnapped by a probable assassin?"

"You're doing the right thing, if my opinion's worth anything," Lyons declared quietly. "Stall it all you can. Maybe. . . ."

"Maybe what?" the Captain asked, ready to accept any gleam of hope.

"I don't know. Just maybe."

"If Tony Danger turns up dead, I don't know . . . either. The only prayer I know, Lyons, is the 23rd Psalm. And somehow it just doesn't seem to fit this problem."

The old boy was really taking it hard.

Carl Lyons understood. Perfectly. You put your life into a job—you worked it and sweated it with every damned thing you had—and the only time anybody ever noticed you was when you stubbed your toe and fell, face-first. Yeah, he understood.

The deputy-chief arrived, followed moments later by the chief himself.

A reporter from the *San Diego Union,* probably picking up the vibrations of something hot, tried to get in. He was all but *thrown* back out.

The battery of lawyers representing the Lucasi bunch were still out there beyond those doors, raising hell louder and louder and demanding to know what was going on.

At almost exactly twenty minutes after the awful event, the duty warden looked up from a phone call he'd just answered and called out, "Is there a Sergeant Carl Lyons in here?"

There was.

But who the hell would be calling him *here?*

Who the hell even *knew* that he was . . . oh hell, it couldn't be.

In a tight voice he told Captain Tatum, "Don't cancel any bets," and stepped forward to take the call.

Yeah, God was still in heaven.

It was Bolan, sounding sober and troubled as he announced, "I've got Tony Danger, Lyons."

He threw an eye signal to Tatum as he replied, "Man, you know how to hurt, don't you. Never mind the throat, just rip the heart out."

That flinty voice told him, "Tell your buddies not to worry. I'll take good care of their prisoner. Just borrowed him for awhile."

"You better tell 'em yourself. Here, I'll—"

"No wait, Lyons. I'm almost ready to pass this town. But first I have to set something up. As long as you're around. . . ."

The Sergeant chuckled drily. "You know I can't—"

"You can this one. Listen to it, anyway."

"I'm going to put another man on the line with us, Mack. Cap'n Tatum, Homicide. Good man, take my word for it."

"All right, but shake it. I'm on short numbers."

Tatum was already at the extension phone. He took Lyons' nod and picked it up. "Tatum, Homicide," he announced. "Is that you, Mack Bolan?"

The Captain's eyes lifted to Lyons as that steely other voice vibrated the receivers, some indefinable emotion registering there in that locked gaze —not awe exactly, but something closely approaching it. Tatum was a cop who could respect greatness, under the law or not.

"It's me. Sorry if I shook your cage. I'd rather

not. I'll return your prisoner as soon as he gives me what I need. An hour, maybe. Two at the most. Meanwhile I need something from your end. Soon as I get it, I'll pass this town. Didn't want to come here in the first place. Good town, San Diego. But you're infected with the creeping rot. I wouldn't even know where to begin carving it out. But I'm going to tip the bucket. It's up to you if it becomes a flood or not."

"Wait," Tatum rasped. "Let's talk about Tony Dan—"

"You wait," the frigid voice snapped back. "The mob boys in your town are second stringers. There's not a *Capo* among them, not even a serious pretender. Your real trouble is in your environment, and I'm not talking about air pollution. You've got a community structure that allows second-stringers like Lucasi and Tony Danger to get a strangle-hold on everything that's good here. Are you with me, Tatum?"

"I'm following you," the Captain replied, almost meekly.

Lyons could not believe it. The big tough cop was standing there getting a lecture, even responding to it with humility. Well, maybe he had it coming and knew it. He *was* a big man.

Bolan was telling him, "One of your proudest citizens—Maxwell Thornton. He's not the great white father he's cracked up to be. He's a sick, miserable, harried man. The mob has the spurs in him, and they're riding the guy into the mud. Maybe he deserves it, but San Diego doesn't."

"Yes," Tatum commented quietly. "Thornton is an important cog in our little overgrown country-

153

club here. He's been accused of rawhiding business practices but. . . ."

"But nothing. He's covered with dirt. You'd be doing the guy a favor to bust him. One-to-five is a better rap than the one he's serving now. Okay, Thornton isn't the only one, but he'd be the crack in the dam. Get him, and all the other dirty straights will fall through the hole. When that happens, Lucasi and company will be out of business in this town. That's all I want. Scratch my back, Tatum, and I'll pass your town."

"All right," the Captain replied soberly. "Tell me where the itch is."

Bolan began the telling, but Lyons only half-heard. The marvel was not the story that Mack Bolan was revealing.

The marvel was that big tough rawhide cop, who was standing there like an adolescent boy receiving the first full course in sex education from a dad who did not believe in pulling punches, a boy with eyes opened wide in wonderment and fascination and awe . . . afraid to believe and afraid not to, daring to hope and hoping to dare.

Yeah.

Lyons could say it with a certainty now.

Mack Bolan was a guy who made his own odds.

When the conversation was ended, Tatum stepped over to the duty desk and told the warden, "Just hang onto those receipts, Tom. And log out Tony Danger. Show him released to his own recognizance, as of the time of those receipts."

The jailor looked dumbfounded, but he nodded his head in understanding.

Then the Captain grabbed Carl Lyons by the arm and propelled him toward the big office at the end of the hall. "Time for the summit conference," he declared in a heavy voice.

"What's the play?" Lyons wanted to know.

"Maybe I'm crazy—or maybe I *was* crazy. Anyway, we're releasing that pack of filth. They'll get no protection from the law in *this* town. They made their lousy bed, now they can die in it."

"You don't mean that," Lyons feebly protested.

"The hell," Captain Tatum said, "I don't."

Yeah. That guy also wrote his own numbers.

17: TRAP PLAY

Tony Danger was bound, gagged and curled into the cramped luggage compartment of the foreign sportster—no doubt suffering the intimations of unavoidable death which were far more agonizing than the final act itself could ever be.

Bolan had shed the police uniform and was now rigged for open warfare. A military web-belt encircled the waist of the black combat outfit, supporting the AutoMag's leather plus a variety of personal munitions—among these, several small fragmentation grenades and a couple of firesticks.

The silent black Beretta was slung into a snap-out shoulder rig at his left side. Another belt crossed the chest from the other shoulder, bearing spare clips for the two autos.

It could be a hell of a hot one.

He hoped that Tatum had bought the idea . . .

and that he would find some way to sell it higher-up.

The Ferrari was parked in the shadows of the marina clubhouse at Mission Bay. Bolan had already established the fact that *Danger's Folly* was in her berth and crewed. He glanced at his watch and tried not to fidget . . . the numbers were getting too damned close . . . where the hell was the girl?

The pre-arranged check-in by Blancanales and Schwarz had brought encouraging news.

Schwarz had reported: "Well it's a pretty cold trail, but I think I may have something. Been talking to some of the technicians out at Thornton Electronics. I believe that's where they reassembled the data-link gear. I got a rumble from one of the guys about some rough-terrain vehicles they brought in last month. He said a special crew was working nights only, some secret project, packaging something very mysterious into those vehicles. I didn't want to push it too hard, but I managed to get some approximate dimensions on the vehicles. Enough to say yeah, it could be. Then I picked up some cross-intelligence. Those mobile rigs, if that was them, weren't driven out of there under their own power. They were hauled away in two big vans from Thornton's trucking line. Again, at night and under tight security wraps. I'm following up on that."

"Okay," Bolan had told him. "Play it cool, Gadgets, not too close. If you get in a jam, beep the Politician. My numbers are too tight."

The report from Blancanales was almost as promising. "She's not in very good shape, Sarge. Tore up over Howlie, but it's more than that. She's scared out of her skull. I finally got her opened up enough to admit that it wasn't her that burnt the papers, but she won't say who did. Doesn't trust anybody, she's really frozen. She didn't know that was you, last night, by the way. I guess she's not thinking too clearly, sort of numb from the shoulders up. Know what I mean? I believe I could blast her loose if I could convince her that you're really on the job. I don't suppose you could make it up here?"

Bolan had to tell him, "No, I'm right on the numbers. But turn on a radio or a TV. The press is into it with both feet now. Maybe she'll believe them."

"Good idea."

"Keep your sentinel tuned in. I may want to beep you for a later report. Also stand ready to give Gadgets some close support. He's on a tight one."

"Yeah, I heard."

Twenty minutes had passed since the receipt of those reports. Bolan was getting edgy. Marsha Thornton was five minutes late for their rendezvous.

He got out of the car and went around to check on Tony Danger's air supply. The guy gave him one of those pleading looks when he opened the trunk door, but he seemed to be breathing all right.

Bolan told him, "Pretty soon now, Tony. Then we'll see."

She arrived a minute later, leaving her car in the regular parking area and stumbling breathlessly into the shadows to redeem a raincheck issued to one of the few men who had, lately, treated her with dignity and understanding.

At the moment, Bolan was finding it difficult to go on understanding. She was still wearing the damn bikini, except that she had added a skimpy top to complete the almost non-existent ensemble.

But then she explained, "I'm late, sorry. Max came home, first time this month he's been in by midnight. I had to lie to him. He thinks I'm on the beach."

Bolan told her, "Maybe it was the last lie. Guess that will be up to you. Tony Danger tells me the film is on board the *Folly*. I'll want you to make sure it's the real thing."

"But he told Max he'd sent it to New York."

"Sure, that took the heat off him and put more of a screw into your husband. But a guy like Tony likes to keep his goodies close by. Anyway, he's seen the light, and he wants to let you off the hook." He pulled her to the rear of the car and opened the trunk. "There's your passport from hell," he told her.

She said, "Oh wow," in a voice just a decibel above a whisper.

Bolan instructed her, "Get in the car and sit tight. If you hear a ruckus, take off."

She showed him saucer eyes and a pained smile, then stepped inside the Ferrari.

Bolan hauled his prisoner from the trunk, set him on his feet, then shoved him toward the docks. "Breathe very carefully and live awhile," he suggested.

The *caporegime*, such a strutting peacock a short while earlier, was now at the verge of collapse. These guys sometimes went this way,

159

Bolan reflected. Beneath those cocky, bullyboy exteriors often beat the fluttering heart of a perpetually frightened little kid—born into despair, reared in panic, matured with violence and an outward show of disrespect for everything feared, which meant *every* thing. These were the guys who died blubbering and pleading—because they had found nothing to justify their lives and even less to crown their deaths. It had something to do with visions of immortality, Bolan suspected; these guys had no visions whatever beyond their own grubby little noses.

He had to half-carry, half-shove the terrified prisoner to the docks. As their feet touched the gangway, a soft voice from the *Folly's* deck exclaimed, *"It's that guy!"*

The Executioner's death voice quickly warned those aboard, "Stand loose, sailors. I've got a cannon down your master's throat."

They boarded, Bolan slamming Tony Danger against the cabin bulkhead with a knee in his belly, the muzzle of the Beretta resting directly between the twitching eyes.

He ripped the tape-gag away and commanded, "Tell 'em, Tony."

It took the guy several tries to find his voice. When it came, it was a death rattle. *"Do as he says! Don't dick around!"*

Turtle Tarantini stepped out of the shadows near the main cabin. He was giving Bolan that same fawning look of respect accorded him earlier, under far different circumstances, and it offered Bolan a variation on his numbers.

"Welcome aboard, Mr. Bolan sir," the Turtle greeted him, the voice shaking just a little.

Bolan snapped, "Where's your crew?"

"Right here, sir. Behind me. You better tell 'em it's okay to come out. We're not armed, sir."

"Step forward and stand to the rail for a frisk. I've got nothing hard for you guys, unless you give me something."

The other two showed themselves, moving carefully, then one by one they came to the rail opposite Bolan's position and presented themselves for the weapons shakedown.

Each one he frisked and sent over the gangway with the instructions, "Don't even look back."

Then it was just Mack Bolan and the guy who, with perhaps some weird presentiment, had named this sleek pleasure craft *Danger's Folly.*

The man who had fully learned the true meaning of *folly* was cringing against the cabin bulkhead, wild eyes framed around the black barrel of the Beretta.

Bolan gave him plenty of time to get the feel of imminent death, then he pulled the pistol away and sheathed it. "Get the film," he commanded.

The guy staggered into the main cabin, Bolan close behind. He slid back a wall panel, fumbled with the dial of a safe, and a moment later dropped a small film cannister into Bolan's outstretched hand.

"That's all?" Bolan asked.

"I swear."

"If it's not, I'll be back to see you."

"I *swear!*"

"Let's go," Bolan said.

They returned to the car—Tony Danger puffing and weaving on unsteady legs.

Marsha Thornton stepped out to greet them.

The deadpan gaze slid the full length of Tony Danger and she said, quietly, "Just look at that."

Bolan opened the can of film and passed it over to her. He also handed her a pencil-flash and told her, "Make sure it's the one."

She examined several frames, quickly, distastefully. "Yes. That's it."

"Burn it." He gave her a butane lighter.

"Right here?"

He nodded. "Right here."

She stripped the cannister, unreeling the film into a loose pile on the cement drive.

As she worked at it, Bolan shoved his prisoner to the side of the car and told the girl, "When you get home, tell your husband all about it. Tell him the hold is gone, except what he built himself and wants to keep for himself. But tell him this. If he stays held, I'll have to come back. And I'll have to break all the holds, my own way. Do you understand what I'm saying?"

She murmured, "Yes, I understand."

"Tell him also that I've located the missing radio gear." He glanced at Tony Danger, then placed a cigarette in his mouth and leaned toward the girl to light it. "I'm going to hit it tonight. I'm giving him that much break. He will understand, just tell him that."

Marsha Thornton, not at all deadpanning anything now, assured the Executioner, "I'll tell him. Thanks."

He said, "Stand back. You'll never get it lit that way."

He pulled her aside, thumbed off a firestick, and tossed it into the pile of film.

It went up in a puff of brilliant incandescence,

writing and shriveling into the nothingness from which it had come, and he told the girl with the glowing eyes, "Now take off. And don't look back. Don't ever look back on this."

She brushed his cheek with moist lips and ran toward her own vehicle.

Bolan told Tony Danger, "You're some rotten bastard, you know that?" Then he crammed the guy into the Ferrari and they returned to town in silence.

Bolan pulled up in front of the police station.

The returning prisoner, baffled but uncomplaining, told the big cold guy beside him, "Listen, Bolan, I—"

"Get out of my car, guy," the frosty voice commanded.

Tony Danger got out and the Ferrari shot forward into the night.

A moment later Bolan pressed the call button on his shoulder-phone, summoning the Politician to a conference.

He told him, "Find Gadgets and get on him right away. I fed Tony the bait and dropped him off. It's *All Systems Red* now, so let's get into close order."

"I've got something hot from Lisa Winters," Blancanales reported.

"Save it 'til we regroup. I've got to spring this trap."

"He really went for it, huh?"

"He went for it, all right. With straining ears and licking lips."

"Just don't let him get clean away, Sarge. He's the one that burned Howlin' Harlan."

The Executioner's voice was tensely frosted as it snapped back, "Are you sure of that?"

"As sure as you were that Howlie didn't burn himself," Blancanales replied.

"Okay. Get on trap station. Get Gadgets in with all speed. This one is liable to be just one beat off the numbers."

Damn right.

"This one" would indeed be crowding every number at Bolan's disposal. Plus a few that he hadn't even found yet.

18: RAWHIDE

John Tatum and Carl Lyons were waiting in a darkened vehicle in a stakeout position outside the police building when Bolan dropped his passenger.

Tatum straightened quickly and declared, "There she blows. The Ferrari."

Lyons' attention was riveted to the dishevelled man who had lurched onto the sidewalk. "That's Tony Danger, eh?"

"The one and only." The Captain chuckled. "Looks like he's been through a grinder."

The Ferrari was already gone, taillights faintly twinkling in the distance. "That Bolan's a cool bastard," Lyons commented.

"We'll probably never know just how cool," Tatum said, sighing.

"Look at that. The guy's actually going inside."

"Oh he's strictly legit," the homicide chief said drily. "Wait'll he finds out he was released over an hour ago."

"Just hope he reacts properly."

"He will. I'd have to mark Bolan A-plus on that score, he knows his enemy."

"I'd still quote it at a hundred-to-one," the L.A. cop sniffed.

"No, not that wide. Tony will call his boss as soon as he realizes it's a new game. And then I think it'll go pretty much as Bolan laid it out."

"Hope you realize you're betting a twenty-six-year career on that," Lyons said. "I mean . . . Bolan's some other kind of guy, yeah. But dammit John, he's no superman."

Tatum chuckled. "We seem to have reversed positions," he said. "Relax, Sergeant. You don't have to take the role of devil's advocate. I'm not going off half-cocked."

Lyons laughed self-consciously. "Sorry."

"It's okay. I might have been a Mack Bolan myself, once. Guys like him don't come gift-wrapped from heaven or hell. They're just guys . . . like you, like me. Destiny shapes 'em. Not personal destiny, none of that shit. *Human* destiny. Or, if you'd rather, call it a chance combination of environment and circumstances, coupled with an individual's unique abilities. Bingo, a Mack Bolan appears. I saw a few guys like him . . . in the hellgrounds of Europe, Second World War. Tell the truth, Lyons, I *am* glad the guy came to town. Made me remember."

"Wanta form a fan club?" Lyons asked, grinning.

"I might do that," the Captain replied soberly.

"I, uh, hate to admit that I wasn't really listening when Bolan outlined his game to you. What, uh, what the hell . . . ?"

"It's a simple power sweep," Tatum explained. "Ben Lucasi is a small-potatoes area chief with dreams of empire. What the hell has he got here, really, in a quiet town at the corner of the nation? A bit of border smuggling, maybe a bit of trading in international contraband, close access to the free-wheeling gambling interests in Mexico. Can you build a national empire out of something like that?"

"Not without some hot gimmick," Lyons decided.

"Well, he's found one. Pretty wild idea, really, and pretty daring when you really think about it. I wouldn't think Lucasi was capable of it. But . . . well, Bolan tells me that Big Little Ben is reaching to corner the horsetrack action in this country. I mean the full gambit . . . from bookmaking to layoff books to numbers' lotteries, racing wires, the whole thing."

"How the hell could he manage that?" Lyons muttered thoughtfully. "The mob already has a pretty intricate structure around that business."

"Yeah, but Benny thinks he's found a new wrinkle. One that will put him in undisputed control of a worldwide gambling wire setup. Then the entire complicated U. S. structure will have to come begging to him to get into the big action. Yeah, it's a hot gimmick . . . if he could make it work."

"How *would* he make it work?"

"Some kind of ultra-sophisticated radio gear he's hijacked from the military. Bolan says that one of our leading citizens has dirty fingers over the deal. Guy heads an electronics firm that does government contract work. Bolan says he was strong-armed into the deal, desperately wants out. It's a defense security-violation rap if he gets nailed. That's what I'm pegging my whole interest on. I believe Thornton—he's the guy—I believe he's the key to a lot of infectious corruption we've been noting around town the past few years. If we could get Thornton to bust loose and. . . ."

Lyons observed, "That's not homicide work."

"I'm a cop," Tatum replied quietly.

"Yeah, you are that," the L.A. Sergeant agreed.

"Anyway, there are plenty of unsolved homicides tied into this mess, I'm sure of that."

"I suppose so."

"I know so. Tony Danger there. He's Lucasi's most trusted triggerman. I know that. So do a lot of other people. He's responsible for a dozen or more homicides in my jurisdiction over the past two years. I *know* it. Proving it in a court of law is something else again. So . . . yeah . . . I'm riding the long end of the odds. Maybe something will shake loose from this Bolan blast."

Lyons grinned, keeping a thought to himself. Cap'n Tatum, it seemed, was a total convert. He wasn't the first. Certainly he wouldn't be the last. Mack Bolan's lonely war was becoming less lonely all the time. Give it to the guy, though, he'd built that base of unofficial support all on his own. It was hard to come into contact with the guy and *not* end up cheering him on . . . if only from the sidelines.

"Anyway," Tatum was explaining further, "Bolan was going to let it drop on Tony Danger that he's planning a hit on this radio equipment. He figures it's the one thing that will bring Lucasi out fighting. Hopefully it will panic the guy. He'll rush off to a wild-ass defense of his precious dream. By that time, Bolan will be right on his tail. He'll let Lucasi pinpoint the equipment for him."

"So why aren't we staking out Lucasi ourselves, instead of sitting here waiting for—"

"You said it yourself a minute ago," Tatum growled. "My job is homicide. I'm not running off on any wild-ass federal—"

"*What* homicide?"

"Maxwell Thornton's. Bolan is betting, and I agree, that Lucasi will order Tony Danger to hit Thornton, and quick. He'll be moving everything he's got to keep his game alive. Thornton is his pivot man. And mine. I aim to keep him alive, and I aim to nail Tony Danger once and for all."

"God I wouldn't want to be on your limb," Lyons commented in a hushed voice.

"Neither would I, but I'm there, so shut up."

"One more thing, Cap'n. These guys have tried radio before. They even set up a legit broadcast station in Mexico a few years back to—"

"Didn't work," Tatum snapped. "First of all, anybody could tune into the broadcasts. Nothing exclusive about that. Secondly, the Mexican government shut them down when our feds requested cooperation. This is a whole new wrinkle. It's more exclusive than any telephone wire. Virtually untappable, and—there he is!"

Tony Danger had reappeared at the entrance to the police building. He appeared to be in much better shape, now—cocky, strutting down the street to the corner.

Moments later a heavy black car swung in to the curb. Tony Danger slid in, and the car slid away.

Tatum moved his vehicle smoothly into the flow of traffic and spoke into his microphone. "Hotel One, subject acquired, moving north toward Pacific Highway. Black limousine, tag California niner-zero-four, hotel-delta-tango. All units close per instructions and maintain surveillance. Subject turning west at. . . ."

Lyons unsheathed his service revolver and checked it, then returned it to leather.

He wished, dammit, that they had been on *Bolan* instead of. . . . All the fireworks, he knew, were headed that other way. Cap'n Tatum, the rawhiding total convert, had turned Big Ben Lucasi's fate over to the uncertain mercies of the Executioner.

Yeah. All the fireworks would be running that other way.

19: END OF TRACK

He watched from his eagle's perch as they rolled out of Lucasi's joint—three big limousines—and he gave them plenty of stretch, tracking the three-car procession of headlights through binoculars until they reached Interstate 5 and headed south. Then he made the jump and sent the Ferrari roaring along the interstate route in hot pursuit.

He had them in sight again well ahead of the interchange and casually tracked them through and onto the downtown leg. It was an excellent freeway system, easily carrying the swift-moving traffic in a no-bunch, no-slow flow. It was still early evening, not quite nine o'clock; another of those San Diego Specials, full moon and blankets of stars, a night with plenty of light, kinder to lovers than to warriors . . . but war it had to be— and a one-shot war, at that.

He'd promised the homicide captain that he would pass this town—so it had to be this time, this place, and this circumstance for the Executioner . . . there could be none other.

The enemy procession veered east onto the city-transit leg at Broadway and kept on easterly beyond the Wabash Freeway exit. It was at this point that Bolan established radio contact with his partners.

"Heading east on the Helix," he announced. "Just passed Wabash. Where away?"

Gadgets Schwarz came in immediately. "Bingo. Running true. Look for them to drop out at State 94, thence southeasterly through Spring Valley."

Bolan responded, "Roj."

Blancanales reported, "I'm just a few minutes from that exit. Want me to bird-dog?"

"You clear, Gadgets?" Bolan wanted to know.

"Yeah, no sweat."

"Okay, Pol. Swing up there. Confirm three crew wagons, Lincolns, I think, running in convoy."

"Roj."

It was a tight game of numbers. Bolan was not allowing himself any luxuries where Ben Lucasi was concerned. The guy was wily. Already, it appeared, the convoy had swung far out of its way in transiting the city along the south. They could have much easier cut across on Interstate 8 . . . if indeed they were humping for Route 94. That would be the desert road running past the Sycuan Indian Reservation on the route to Tecate, a Mexican border town. Something rumbled deep in Bolan's memory, then, causing him to again send a query to Gadgets Schwarz.

"Gadgets, you said to look for high ground for

172

these radio links. Doesn't Route 94 head east at the border?"

"Right. My present position is just west of Potrero, which is almost due north of Tecate, just a few miles over the border. You have that on your area map?"

Bolan replied, "Finger right on it. Trace eastward, beyond the Campo Reservation. Looks like a high peak over there."

Schwarz came back: "Right. That would be Tecate Divide, elevation more than four thousand feet. The trailers I've been tracking were parked here near Potrero as recently as today. The track fizzled out right here, though."

"Okay, stay alert. It looks like the play is running your way."

Blancanales checked in a moment later to confirm that assumption. "Right, check three Detroit blacks off the interstate at Spring Valley, running south on 94."

Bolan replied, "Bingo. Fall in behind them and maintain track. I'm coming around."

"You'll have to heat bearings to do it. They're clocking eighty."

"I've got bearings a'plenty," Bolan chuckled. He moved the Ferrari into the upper ranges of the tach and closed quickly to the exit ramp, then rolled carefully through Spring Valley and onto the open road of the desert country. He could see the procession ahead of him, now the only lights on the road.

"Have you in sight," he reported to Blancanales. "Drop back some, Pol. You're crowding them."

"Right. Didn't want to chance losing them going through town. I am easing off now."

A moment later Bolan was running-up onto the rear of the Corvette being piloted by Blancanales.

"Coming around."

"Roj, man—go."

Bolan was burning rubber alongside the Mafia convoy, slumped into the racing backboard of the hot car to conceal his own face but reading occupants as he whizzed past.

"Here's the head count," he reported, when he was well ahead. Rear car, five. Lucasi and bodyguards, looks like. Middle, eight—gun car with jumpseat. Lead car, six. They look tough."

Schwarz immediately checked in. "I'm just dragging down here. Want me to run up to Barrett and pick up on it there?"

Bolan was a full mile ahead of the convoy now. He told Schwarz, "Affirm. Assume station running slowly southward. Make them pass you, then tag along. Pol, you swing ahead at that point. Maintain with their lights just in view behind you."

Both men acknowledged the instructions and Bolan went on to scout the road ahead. He went through Jamul and, six minutes later, the tiny community of Dulzura. Just below that point he passed the warwagon, tooting at Schwarz and receiving a return salute, then burned on southward toward Barrett.

This was rugged country, desolate but pretty in the moonlight, appearing abandoned and hardly touched by the human hand or foot.

A little side road running off eastward a few miles below Dulzura came up in his headlamps. He slowed, overshot the junction, then squealed about in a U-turn and returned for an inspection.

A weathered sign proclaimed that this was the road to Barrett Reservoir.

Bolan found the spot on his area map and closely studied the surrounding countryside. Then he descended from the Ferrari for a closer look at some other kind of signs.

The hunch seemed to be right on-target. Heavy-wheeled vehicles had turned onto that road not too much earlier. He found a place on the turn where a set of double-wheels had slipped off the roadbed into the soft shoulder.

He stood there in the cool night air, allowing his senses to flare and absorb the lie of that place, then he spoke into the shoulder-phone. "Road running east off 94, couple of miles above Barrett. It smells. Map shows possible connection over to U.S. 80. I'm checking it out. Let me know if track runs beyond this point."

Schwarz told him, "It might be hot, Sarge. They've been moving those rigs every few days. And listen, watch it. Guy at a truck stop down near Barrett told me those rigs are not being handled by teamsters. Says it's two guys in each cab and they look mean as hell."

Bolan replied, "Roj, thanks." He returned to the Ferrari and sent it in a dangerously fast acceleration along the little back road.

If it had looked like no-wheres-ville out along the state highway, then this area was strictly twilight zone. Rugged, hilly, wild—with road to match.

It would be rough going for a couple of big semi-trailers. And Bolan's "combat feel" was flowing strong in his veins. If Lucasi had just ordered those rigs a'moving again, after hearing Tony

Danger's report, then . . . yeah, that could be blood he was smelling, for damn sure.

And if Lucasi was in the panic which Bolan had programmed for him then, yeah, he had those rigs rolling while he raced with a gun-convoy to protect the movement.

A few minutes later Bolan knew that he had scored. His heart shifted into combat-pump as he spotted the twin set of headlamps on a curve far ahead, running bumper to bumper, two big diesel rigs laboriously navigating that back-country road.

He announced into his shoulder-phone, "Bingo. I have the target in sight. About . . . halfway to the reservoir. Fall in close and protect my rear."

Schwarz reported, "They just passed me, running hell-bent. Pol is coming around now. Do we hit them out here or allow them to close some first?"

"Let them close," Bolan commanded. "Just stay on their tail. From the moment you hit the turn-off, run dark. There's plenty of visibility out here without lights."

"Affirm."

"Watch it, Sarge," Blancanales growled.

"Name of the game," Bolan replied.

"I'll run on down about a half-mile beyond the junction, then double back."

"Okay," Bolan agreed tightly. "Watch this road. It's a bitch."

He surged forward then, sending the Ferrari into a hot run-up on those lights ahead, then he fell back, tracking at about ten car-lengths.

"Target knows I'm here," he announced. "Report into the junction."

"Roj," from Schwarz.

"Wilco," said Blancanales. "Running past now."

A moment later Schwarz reported, "Convoy turning east."

"Have them in sight," Blancanales muttered. "Coming about and re-closing."

"Tracking eastward," Schwarz said seconds later. "Are you running dark, Pol?"

"Affirm."

"Let's mark positions. Landmark ahead. Falling-down cabin, off to right. Large boulder, scraggly tree in front. Passing . . . right . . . now, *mark!*"

Ten seconds later, Blancanales reported, "Mark. I'm off you ten seconds."

"Run it there," Bolan instructed.

So there was the line-up. Two diesel rigs, moving slowly hardly a car-length apart, Bolan pacing them ten car-lengths back. About two miles back and moving up fast, the three crew wagons, bearing a total of nineteen guns. A few seconds to their rear and running dark, Schwarz in the war-wagon; ten seconds behind him, Blancanales.

Tight numbers, yeah . . . *damn* tight.

Bolan waited until the lights of the crew wagons were showing behind him. They would be spotting him now, running just off their precious cargo, wondering and fuming . . . "Didn't that damn sports car pass us back there a few miles?"

He was watching also the terrain ahead and to either side of the line of travel. A most advantageous spot was coming up, just ahead, where the road threaded low ground between pressing hillocks.

He released a fragmentation grenade from his combat belt, pulled the pin, and announced into the shoulder-phone, "Going!"

The Ferrari surged forward and up along the left flank of the mobile targets. He leaned across the seat and waved at the guys in the rear truck then moved smoothly on to run abreast of the lead tractor, tensely counting his numbers, pacing the targets into the needle, sliding far to the right and steering with his left hand . . . and then the numbers were all used up.

The driver of the target vehicle was shouting something at him as he flipped the grenade, out and up, right into the guy's lap.

At that same instant he swung back to the controls of the Ferrari and sent her screaming ahead, putting three seconds of distance between himself and that doomed semi.

One of those frozen instants of time descended, a stretched-out and seemingly infinite *present*, with *past* forever behind and *future* looming threateningly and yet unapproachable.

The driver of that leading crew wagon had already gotten the smell and was pressing forward, leading the other two cars into a wild pass around the rear truck.

The flash of the explosion illuminated Bolan's cockpit and cast red streamers into his rear-view mirror. Something metallic whizzed past his open window and showering glass overtook him and rained on him.

The big rig weaved and veered off to the left, tried to climb the high ground over there and failed, jack-knifed, slid along on screaming rubber, overturned with a crashing-roaring-grinding and burst into flames.

The immediate aftermath of that event was

sheer pandemonium. Two crew wagons and another big rig plowed into that mess, with a whole new ball game of screaming rubber, crumpling and rending metal, shoestring explosions, fireballs, the screams and shouting of men trapped in that *immovable present.*

Bolan's Ferrari had already come about and raced onto the high ground overlooking the hit site. He was grounded and commanding into his shoulder-phone, "Close with all speed," when the survivors down there began staggering clear of the fantastic pile-up.

The rear crew-wagon had careened into a broadside halt across the road, practically roasting in the white-hot heat of the gasoline-fed fires.

Guys were scrambling out of there and waving choppers around, looking for something to shoot at. Bolan recognized Lucasi's big house captain, the Diver. He was yelling at two other guys, *"Cover our rear!"*

Bolan gave them something more pressing to cover, sighting down with the impressive Auto-Mag, squeezing off three deliberate rolling booms, seeking and finding an ignition point beneath the engine hood of that as-yet undamaged vehicle. He got an ignition and a small fireball which quickly whoofed into the fumes blanketing that area, following immediately with a full-scale explosion which lifted the heavy vehicle clear of all four wheels and resettled it at an entirely different angle, engulfed in flames.

A human torch was staggering around down there near the spot where he'd last noted the Diver; Bolan felled him with a mercy-round near the top of the torch. This drew immediate return fire from two heavy choppers which sliced up the embankment just below his feet; then the lighter snare drum-roll of machine pistols entered the argument as Blancanales and Schwarz acquired station.

Bolan left the remainders to them.

But for one.

Big Little Ben Lucasi was on his knees at the side of the road, blood trickling down the side of his neck, tormented eyes gazing with disbelief at the flames and wreckage marking the final disposition of his late-budding bid for international importance.

Bolan walked slowly down the embankment to stand over the little would-be *Capo*. He said, coldly, "You crapped out, Lucasi."

The glazed eyes shifted slowly to the tall figure in black which towered above him. They shrank, then blazed again in a curious mixture of defiance and defeat.

"I knew you'd get to my territory sooner or later," Lucasi muttered. "So go ahead. Kill me."

Bolan replied, "All right."

And he did so, the muzzle of the AutoMag making contact with Big Ben's little skull at that critical point directly between the eyes. He squeezed off once, sending 240 shattering grains exploding into that corruption, at a muzzle energy of a thousand or so foot-pounds.

Odds and ends of bone and brains flew off into that immovable moment and what was left of Big Ben Lucasi was sent backwards for a slide into the spreading flames.

Bolan holstered the AutoMag and spoke to the flames.

"Goodbye, Howlie," he said quietly. *"Bon voyage."*

EPILOGUE

The three warriors regrouped at the front fender of the Ferrari as the flames below were burning themselves out.

Gadgets Schwarz quietly commented, "End of track. I defy anyone to say even what was in those trucks."

Bolan said, "Just as well. It's a decent place for a burial."

Blancanales told them, "It doesn't end here, though. It's what I've been wanting to report. Lisa Winters told me that Tony Danger had them all over a barrel. Something about a wild party on a yacht, and some pictures Tony was holding over their heads. She said—"

"It figures," Bolan interrupted tiredly. "The messes people make of their lives."

Blancanales said, "Well now wait. Tony Danger

is the guy that blasted the colonel. He went out there to make a swap, supposedly. Howlie was going to turn over the records on that missing gear in exchange for those pictures. Instead, he blasted the colonel and burnt the papers. I guess Howlie went down fighting, though. It was his own gun that did him in. I think he was planning a little surprise play of his own. Lisa said they were fighting over this gun . . . it turned out to be the colonel's. Anyway—"

"Anyway he's dead and gone," Bolan said. "And the game *is* over. I already consigned Tony Danger to the San Diego cops, for better or for worse. And I—"

"That part's over too," Schwarz put in. "I was monitoring the police frequencies. Heard it while I was coasting along Highway 94. Shoot-out at Maxwell Thornton's house. Police trap. Tony Danger is dead, two other contractors critically wounded."

Bolan sighed and thumbed reloads into his AutoMag's clip. "So it's fully ended," he said wearily. "I believe Thornton will take my deal. Especially after. . . ."

Blancanales was staring at the pile of destruction just below them. He said, "Yeah. So where to, now?"

Bolan gave him a surprised look. He said, "I was on my way to Philly when I received your message."

"What's going in Philly?"

"A guy named Angeletti."

Blancanales whistled. *"That* guy. It's going to be a mean one, Sarge. Gadgets and I can—"

"You can go home," Bolan said firmly. "I have to work Philly on my own."

The two death-squaders understood.

Schwarz said, "You know how to reach us, any time you need to."

Bolan replied, "Sure. You guys hang loose. It's been, uh, like old times."

"Sure has," Schwarz agreed.

Blancanales whipped off a fat money-belt and thrust it at the Executioner. "The war chest," he said. "Not much gone. All I bought was the gear for Gadgets and the Corvette."

Bolan didn't even look at it. He growled, "Keep it. All I want is what I can carry in my pocket. I pick it up as I need it."

Schwarz grinned. "I guess your credit's always good, eh? How much have you banged the mob for, so far?"

Bolan smiled back. "Millions, I guess. Who counts? Easy come, easy go—right?"

"Well," Blancanales drawled, "I guess we better...."

Bolan said, "Set yourselves up in business."

"What?"

"Use the war chest as a stake. Face it, you guys are living on the heartbeat, anyway. Right? Make it pay."

"What sort of business?" Schwarz asked, interested.

"You'll think of something fitted to your talents." Bolan shrugged. "I can think of a couple right off the top. Industrial counter-intelligence. Large services to small nations. You've got the smarts. And if that's what you like best . . ."

The two men exchanged glances. A world of ideas met in that interchange of minds.

Blancanales said, "Just the same, if you ever need us . . ."

Bolan grinned, shook their hands, and told them, "Split, will you? Keep the warwagon, Gadgets. I'll pick up another somewhere."

And that was the end of another brief partnership.

Blancanales and Schwarz trudged past the smouldering remains of the San Diego Siege, got into their vehicles, and headed west—into only God knew what.

Mack Bolan, forever *the Executioner*, pointed his Ferrari to the east. Somewhere over there was a U. S. highway . . . and somewhere beyond that lay another hell called Philadelphia.

Howlin' Harlan, some nice people, and a fine old city he'd been glad to pass over, lay behind him.

Stretched out ahead was an infinity which the Executioner had come to think of as his "wipe-out trail" . . . and an eternity which he had long ago identified as hell.

A guy would have to be insane to keep on with this.

But, then, he'd have to be dead not to.

Bolan grinned at the eastern horizon without humor, and, half-aloud, told himself, "Right on, man."

Philly was going to be a cold one.

PINNACLE BOOKS

THE INCREDIBLE ACTION PACKED SERIES

DEATH MERCHANT

His name in Richard Camellion, he's a master of disguise, deception and destruction. He does what the CIA and FBI cannot do. They call him THE DEATH MERCHANT!

Order	Title	Bool No.	Price
_____	#1 The Death Merchant	PO21N	95¢
_____	#2 Operation Overkill	PO85N	95¢
_____	#3 The Psychotron Plot	P117N	95¢

and more to come . . .

PINNACLE BOOKS

Violence is
a man!
His name is
Edge...

The bloodiest action-series ever published, with a hero who is the meanest, most vicious killer the West has ever seen.

It's sharp —
It's hard —
It's EDGE

GEORGE G. GILMAN